The Light

GAIL PATE

PAGE PUBLISHING, INC.
New York, NY

First originally published by Page Publishing, Inc. 2016

ISBN 978-1-68409-403-5 (Paperback)
ISBN 978-1-68409-404-2 (Digital)
ISBN 978-1-68409-462-2 (Hardcover)

Printed in the United States of America

"Trust me," he said as I let him take my hand and place it on his heart.

"I feel normal to you?" he asked and pressed my hand harder against his chest. "Does this feel normal to you?" He leaned forward and kissed me.

I looked at him standing there in the moonlight, and it was if my eyes began to blur.

"Trust me," he said again as his body began to … began to become—I don't know—a light of some kind, a vapor of some sort of energy.

Sixteen-year-old Christi Randolph was looking forward to a week of normalcy at the beach house with her Aunt Abby, a place she loved and felt like she belonged to. Little did she know, this week would be anything but normal.

The Light is a teen sci-fi novel unfolding a mystery with a touch of romance that will leave the reader wanting to see what happens next.

For my luvy and sweetums.
You are a light in my life, and I love
you to the moon and back.

PART I

Chapter One

"Are you buckled in?"

"Luvy?" My Aunt Abigail was so predictable I did not even have to take my headphones off to know what she was asking me. I smiled, nodded, and tightened my belt and settled in for the flight. It had already been a very busy morning. My dad had brought me to the airport to meet Aunt Abby, and as usual, we were running late. "Dad, I do believe that you will be late for my wedding when I get married … someday, that is."

"Well, my darling daughter, since we don't have to worry about that until you are at least forty, help me get these bags out to the car, and we will be on our way."

My dad still treats me like his little girl even though I turned sixteen on my last birthday. Most of the time, I love that about him, but sometimes I feel like I'm the adult. Like when we arrived at the airport, he got teary eyed before we even got parked.

"Dad, it's only for a week, and I've gone with Aunt Abby to the beach this week every year now for the last six years."

"I know, honey … I just miss you already."

"Dad," I said as I leaned over and kissed his cheek, "I'll miss you too. Now let's hurry."

I spotted Aunt Abby first; she was already reading a book she had brought for our time on the beach. Some uplifting, soul-searching, inspirational novel that she had picked up at the airport bookstore probably. She saw us just as we started to approach where she was sitting. "Luvy! Oh, I'm so glad to see you and your dad." She hugged us both and then gathered her bags, and we headed toward the security checkpoint. "Call me when you land, honey."

"I will, Dad. I love you."

"Love you too."

"See you in a week! We'll have a great time!" Aunt Abby said as she hugged my dad and then turned to take a place in line. I followed, not turning back because I knew my dad would have tears running down his cheeks. He would watch us until he could no longer see us. Just as we were about to make the turn to the security scanners, I couldn't resist. I turned and looked toward the spot we had left him. He was there watching. Our eyes met; his were wet with tears. I gave him a quick wave, and I was next in line to be scanned. I would not see him for a week. I would miss him, but I had been waiting for this week all spring, and now it was here. It will be a great week just like Aunt Abby had said.

As I put my shoes, watch, iPod, and jewelry in the tray to be scanned, I regretted wearing all the bracelets. I had forgotten about them really. They were a collection of bead strands, bands, and chains that had been gifts. It was easier to just take them all off than to just undo the metal ones. So with some effort, I slid them off my wrist and into the tray. Aunt Abby followed me, and we collected our trays and looked for an open bench to sit and put ourselves back together, when just as I turned after having picked up my tray, I was bumped from behind, and my tray went flying, with the contents scattering all along the floor in front of me.

"Can't you watch where you are going?" I asked as I dove to the floor, picking up the pieces scattered everywhere.

"Oh, my goodness, Luvy," Aunt Abby said as she sat her tray down and helped me pick up bracelets that had been slung her way.

"Sorry," I heard him say. "Let me help you."

"No ... I've got it!" I snapped. That tone was not like me; I'm really not sure why I acted that way. Maybe my emotions were just on edge. I never even looked up to see the idiot who had just started my day off so well. I did, however, notice his T-shirt as he stooped down for his unsuccessful attempt to help.

A Michigan logo. Go figure, I thought as Aunt Abby handed me the last beaded one.

"Everything okay?" asked the TSA officer, as he had come over to see why two people were on their hands and knees holding up the line exiting the security area.

"Yes, sir. Just a little mishap," said Aunt Abby. "Thank you. Let's go, Luvy." She continued as we headed down the corridor to the gate area.

"I hope we got all of them," I said.

"I'm sure we did," Aunt Abby said. "But you can double-check when we get to the gate."

I had stuck all of them into the side pocket of my carry-on. I'm sure we did, but I would feel better after I checked. We found a seat at the boarding area, and I began to pull them out and slip them back on.

"Oh no!" I said as I felt frantically into the zippered compartment and found it to be empty. "The one my mom gave me ... it's missing! I will be back!" I said as I started to run back down the hall toward the screeners.

"Luvy! You'll miss the flight!" I heard Aunt Abby say as I dashed down the corridor, still carrying my bag and the coffee Aunt Abby had gotten me before we had gotten to the gate. I don't know why I grabbed them! So Aunt Abby wouldn't have to deal with them I guess. Anyway, I ran as fast as I could, dodging other passengers heading to their gates, readjusting the strap of my carry-on on my shoulder as I ran, looking for a trash can to throw the coffee. I heard my cell phone ring just as I approached the screening area.

Probably Aunt Abby, I thought as I dug into my carry-on. While still in full stride, I looked down to find my phone and ran into something or someone, and the coffee I was still carrying all dumped down the front of me, and the empty cup landed on the floor at my feet. *Unbelievable!* I thought. *Could this day get any worse?*

It was then I saw the shirt—that Michigan logo shirt worn by the klutz that had just run into me … again!

"What is it with you? Is it your mission in life to ruin mine? Look at me!" I had wet coffee stains all down the front of my new white outfit. "And I've lost a bracelet! Thanks to you!" I said as I moved around him and started down the corridor, leaving the mess on the floor. He could clean it up or not. I didn't have time; I had to find it! My mom had given me that bracelet … I had to find it!

"I have it!"

"What?" I thought as I froze in my tracks and slowly turned to face the sole reason my heart was racing and the fact I felt like screaming.

"I have it!" he said again, and then I saw it dangling from between his thumb and index finger, as I slowly walked back to where he stood. I truly didn't know if I wanted to hug him or hit him with both fists. "I knew you would come back to find it. I found it after you left, but I didn't see which direction you went. So I waited for you. If I had not found you, I would have left it with security. But I knew you would come back for it."

I heard what he was saying to me, but I did not even look at him. This moron of a Michigan guy … I was so relieved, mad, disgusted, wet, and coffee-stained that I grabbed the bracelet from his grip and picked up the empty cup off the floor and headed back to the boarding gate without even a thanks to him.

"You're welcome!" he called out to me. "And the name suits you!"

Moron! I thought again as I started to run toward the gate. Aunt Abby would be waiting, and we could put this awful beginning to the day behind us.

"You found it?" she asked as I fell into the seat beside her. Other passengers were beginning to board. We would be called soon.

"Yes!"

"Thank goodness!" we both said at the same time. We smiled at each other, and I latched the bracelet around my wrist. It was my favorite one. As I looked at it, I thought of his words: "The name suits you." *Princess*, the simple gold chain read—my mom's princess. I looked at the words that the gold links spelled out and rubbed my finger across them. I missed my mom so much.

"That's us, Luvy," Aunt Abby said as she rose and gathered her bag. After boarding and settling in for the flight, I tightened my belt, closed my eyes, and sang the words to the song playing on my iPod to myself. It would be a two-hour flight and then an hour's drive to the beach house in South Carolina. Maybe I would sleep … it had been a hectic morning.

Sleep I did not! "The name suits you!" I kept hearing his sarcastic remark in my head. I had been rude, but he had no right to judge me. After all, he ran into me! He deserved the tone I spoke to him. Well, not *spoke*, really.

The words were directed *at* him, but we had no conversation. Then why couldn't I get what he said out of my brain? I turned the music up a little louder; maybe that would drown it out.

My mom had given me the bracelet before she left for Wyoming. I don't know what I would have done if I had lost it. My thoughts drifted to the day my mom had given the bracelet to me. She and my stepdad, Tom, were packed and leaving for Wyoming.

"Why do you have to move there?"

"Honey, you know we have to go. The ranch has been in Tom's family for generations. You could change your mind and go with us."

"I'm not leaving in the middle of a school year, Mom. Besides, who wants to live in Wyoming?"

"Christi, you know Poppie needs us to come."

Poppie is what I called Tom's dad. He had been that since my mom and Tom had gotten married five years ago. We had visited the ranch several times. I loved the visits, but to live there? It was in the middle of nowhere. Nothing but cows and horses. The horses I loved! For a city girl, I could ride pretty well. But Tom hadn't lived there since he left for the army years ago. Poppie had been sick for the past couple of years. He couldn't keep up the ranch, so Tom felt he had to go help.

"We can't lose the ranch, honey. Tom loves that place. We love that place. You can come as soon as school is out for the summer. You know that is not my preference, but your dad and I have agreed that you can finish the school year out. I'll come get you as soon as you can pack when school is out."

"I don't want to move there, Mom. My friends are here. I have swimming …"

"You will make new friends, and they have swim teams there."

"Yeah … farm ponds," I said under my breath.

"Honey, you love Poppie, and we always have a great time when we visit. Anyway, we have talked about this. You'll have a great spring break with Abby, and the rest of the school year will fly by. It will be summer before we know it. We will get settled in, your room will be all ready for you."

"Mom, you can go if you want to … I'm not! Dad said I can stay as long as I want to! I'm not going!"

I ran out of the room, up the stairs, and slammed my bedroom door. She couldn't make me go. I was sixteen. I could make my own decisions. I laid on my bed, the only piece of furniture left in my room. Everything else had been moved into the U-Haul. Our whole house was being packed into the U-Haul, and the next morning, I would go to my dad's. And my mom and Tom would head west. I knew they had to go. Poppie needed Tom, and my mom loved Tom. She had to go. It wasn't easy for her to leave. My dad and her being friends since the divorce made it easier for her though. Staying with my dad, I could stay at my school, finish my commitment to the swim team, and besides, I loved being at my dad's.

Oh no! I had not called my dad back. He had called me at the airport when the moron ran into me, and everything had happened so quickly I had forgotten to call him back.

"What is it, Luvy?" Aunt Abby asked.

"My dad. I need to call him back." I started to dig into my carry-on for my phone.

"You'll have to wait until we land, Luvy. You can't use your phone in flight. We'll be landing shortly."

Great, I thought and stuffed my phone back into the bag. She was right. I no more than closed my eyes, and we were on the ground. As we taxied to the gate, I gave my dad a quick call to let him know that we were fine and would see him in a week.

As I waited for Aunt Abby to sign for a rental car, I texted my mom and asked her to give my love to Poppie and hoped he was doing better. As I hit Send, I wondered if she would even get a signal with her cell phone in the middle of cow country! Probably not!

"Okay, Luvy! We are ready!"

"We are!" I said. "For a great week!" I took her arm, and we laughed as we walked out the terminal to the car they had waiting for us.

"Your dad tells me you are going to stay with him this summer. How does your mom feel about that?" Aunt Abby asked as we pulled away from the terminal.

"Not just for the summer," I said. "I'm not moving out there ... away from all of my friends, all my commitments, my dad, you. I'm not!"

"What about your mom, Luvy? It will break her heart not having you there."

"Then she didn't have to go! I'm not going to move out there! She can't make me! I'm old enough to decide."

"Okay, Luvy. We don't have to talk about it. I'm sure you will do the right thing, what is best for the whole family. What do you want to do this week? Do you still want to take the Junior Lifeguard training? It is this week, remember?"

"Cool … yeah, that will be great. And then just hang out."

"We will certainly do that, and we'll fit in some fun stuff too!"

Aunt Abby and I always have fun together not doing anything. We talk and laugh about the silliest things. We just get each other. Even when it doesn't make sense to anyone else, we get it. This was our week, just the two of us. No worries. No sadness. Just laughing and good times, just like we always have when we are together. Oh yeah, and there is the beach! We'd been coming here since I was little, but for the last couple of years, it had been just Aunt Abby and me. Girl bonding time, she calls it. I just loved being with Aunt Abby anywhere, so it was going to be a great week!

"Are we there yet?" I asked, knowing exactly how long it took us to drive to the beach house.

"Almost." Aunt Abby reached over and patted my head. "I'm glad you are here, Luvy."

"I love you, Aunt Abby." I said.

"I know you do, Luvy. But I love you more!"

After a quick stop to pick up some groceries, we finally arrived. "Look, Luvy, the Carltons are already here." The Carltons were friends of Aunt Abby's and Uncle John's and next-door neighbors here in South Carolina. I had seen them a few times.

"I think they have someone staying with them. He is signed up for lifeguarding too. It will be nice for you to know someone."

"I don't know him, Aunt Abby."

"You will. We are having them for lunch tomorrow," she said as we started to carry groceries out of the car.

"Great! Can't wait!"

Aunt Abby laughed as we walked up the stairs to the beach house. I loved it here. I loved the smell of the ocean. I loved the feel of the sand under my feet. I loved the memories I had here. I glanced over at the Carltons. Yes, they were there. The sure sign that they were there was flying high. The flag they always put up as soon as they arrived. A big ugly blue and gold flag, and after today, I despised it even more ... a Michigan flag! I really hoped the jerk from this morning had missed his flight and would have a miserable spring break. Maybe he would go spelunking in a cave somewhere. Somewhere he had no contact with people!

Ugh. It frustrated me to think about it, but enough of that. We were here, the place that I loved, and it would be a great week of fun and sun with Aunt Abby. And I was not going to think of dealing with my mom and Wyoming for at least one week!

As we carried in the last of the groceries, the ocean waves welcomed us. I would sleep with the window open tonight for sure!

Chapter Two

It was the smell of the coffee that woke me. Seven fifteen and Aunt Abby was already up, probably on her second cup of coffee. I threw the covers off and headed lazily downstairs and could hear Aunt Abby talking as I entered the kitchen. She had her arm around a lady I recognized to be Nancy Carlton, and they both appeared to be crying.

"Abby, what's happening?" I asked.

"Hey, Luvy, you remember Mrs. Carlton?

"Yes, hello, Mrs. Carlton," I said as I walked over to them.

"Hi, Christi. I'm glad you are here with Abby this week. You will have a wonderful time. Thanks, Abby," she said as she stood to leave. "Thanks for listening. I have to go … rain check on lunch? We will talk later."

"No problem," said Aunt Abby as she followed her to the door. "Let me know if I can help in any way."

"I will … bye, Christi!"

"Bye, Mrs. Carlton," I called to her, puzzled by what had taken place.

"It's Bob, Luvy. He had a stroke and is confined to a wheelchair. It happened over the winter. Poor Nancy. She wanted them to come anyway. It has always been their tradition since their kids were little."

I remembered Bob Carlton. "That is so sad," I said. "He would always help me with my sand castles when I was little. Poor Mrs. Carlton. How can she manage by herself?"

"She will have to have help," Abby said. "She wants him to enjoy some of the same things he has always enjoyed here at the beach, but some things are just not possible right now."

"Will he ever walk again?"

"They don't know, Luvy. That is what they are praying for."

"That is so sad," I repeated as I poured myself a cup of coffee. Aunt Abby and I had been drinking coffee together since I was three. Well, at first it was imaginary. But for real since I was eleven. She says it is one of the little pleasures in life. I mostly like it because she does. And with sugar and cream … it is pretty good!

"I checked the calendar, and after breakfast, you should head on down to sign up for class. It is at the life-guard stand just up the beach. They have your name—you just need to check in really. It says 10:00 a.m. The weather is great, so you might get there early in case they have more kids than spots."

"OK. I have time to sit with you for a while," I said as we moved toward the huge porch that faced the ocean.

"We are so blessed, Christi. We should never take a day for granted. Promise me you will always be happy and not regret one single day, Luvy!" Aunt Abby looked so sad that it almost made me cry.

"You are making me sad right now," I said as I hugged her. "I can check on the Carltons later if you want me to."

"She will let us know if she needs us. Maybe we will stop by tomorrow. You don't worry, and don't forget to call your mom. She said she would like to hear your voice and not just get a text."

"I'll call her before I head out," I replied. "Guess I will eat some breakfast and shower."

"K … I am just going to sit here for a while," Aunt Abby said.

"Refill on your coffee?" I asked as I stood to go inside.

"I'm good, thank you, Luvy. Love you."

"To the moon and back!" I said, closing the screen door behind me.

The conversation with my mom had been short and not sweet. She just does not get it.

"The school is great out here," she had said.

"Wonderful. What does that have to do with me?" I asked sarcastically.

"You will change your mind when you get here, honey. Can't wait. Everyone sends their love."

"Gotta go, Mom."

"Love you," she said.

"Me too."

I was approaching the lifeguard stand and could see that Aunt Abby was right; there were a lot of kids there already.

"Christi Randolph," I said to the lifeguard at the sign-in table, and she checked off my name on the roster. "How many spots are going to be filled?" I asked as I surveyed the dozen or so who were congregating around the station.

"Only four," she replied. "We will begin as soon as Ben gets here."

"Who's Ben?" I asked.

"The lead lifeguard."

"Oh." I stepped aside and started to size up the other applicants there to partner with one of the lifeguards for the week. I had been shadowing for three summers now, so I hoped that would help me gain a spot. Not to mention that I was the captain of my swim team back home. I had the fastest lap times of the whole team. My mom says I've always been a fish and I've always loved being in the water. It was so quiet and peaceful. I knew that would help me in the relay. The ocean was beautiful, even more than usual. This morning, it seemed as if the sun glistened on the waves. A few people were out collecting shells that were washed ashore from the tide, and heads dotted the water with tourists who couldn't wait to feel the waves, laughing and talking; it really was a perfect way to start the day. I could see why Aunt Abby was going to move here. *Better than Wyoming*, I thought to myself.

"Okay, everybody. Huddle up!" I heard someone say.

Huddle up, I thought. *This is not football.* I turned and joined the group that was being addressed by the lead lifeguard.

"Hey, guys! My name is Ben. I'm the lead for the week. As I call out your name, let's line up in two rows, alternating until all names are called. We will only have four juniors, and we have fourteen signed up, so the relays will be elimination until we have four."

As the group started to gather around the lead who was speaking, his back was to me, and my first thought was he looked like a football player: muscular, tall, tan. Did I mention muscular? As he began to call out names and people began to line up, he turned my direction, and out of his mouth, he said, "Randolph, Christi?" I just stood there, stunned. He scanned the remaining ones of us not yet called.

"Christi Randolph?" he said again.

"I'm here," I managed to squeak out and stepped around people to take my place in one of the lines.

"Nice you could join us!" he said, and called out the next name on the list.

Unbelievable! Standing in front of me, the lead lifeguard whom I was to shadow all week, the week I had been looking forward to all winter in my ever-changing life, the one thing that contained no stress, this …this … *Ben* was none other than the moron from the airport. Mr.

Michigan, idiot klutz … how could this be? Maybe I was still in bed and this whole morning had been a dream. He was still talking. I was not hearing anything. I couldn't focus … I couldn't hear … I felt like I was going to faint. *Breathe, just breathe,* I told myself. *You will wake up any moment.*

"Randolph! Are you in or not?"

I was snapped back to reality, and it was not a dream. I would never forget the face of the moron, and he was again standing in front of me, looking right at me, barking orders at me … and seemingly not remembering me at all. Maybe his ruining people's days was so common that he could not possibly remember all his victims.

"Oh … I'm in," I said in a tone that was more of a challenge than a statement.

"Great!" he responded and walked ahead to again address the group.

How could he not remember me? And how was he here—the very beach, the very spot that I was? Maybe he was following me? A stalker? A killer? This could not just be a coincidence. This didn't even happen in the movies … should I leave, tell Aunt Abby of this weird guy whom I had encountered at the airport and who had now just shown up here? No, he would not cheat me out of this week. And if he really didn't remember me, by the end of the week, he would … I would see to it!

The relay started with running in sand that was so deep it was halfway up our calves. Forty yards down and back—it eliminated half the people. The winner of that relay would advance to the water relays. I was one of the eight who advanced into my strongest events … the water.

The relays were set up in lanes marked in the water by ropes and buoys with two floating platforms that a lifeguard was stationed on. One was halfway out, about twenty-five yards, and another about fifty yards out. We were to swim out and back. The winner was to advance to the last and most difficult—the weighted water relay.

"First up, Randolph/Wilson—out and back, minimum time applies. On my start …"

I stepped forward to stand beside Eric Wilson, a skinny kid who appeared to be about my age. *Piece of cake*, I thought to myself. "I hear Michigan finished last in the Big Ten in swimming last year!" I said as I stood waiting for the Start command.

"I don't know … I don't live in Michigan," said Eric Wilson, looking at me with a puzzled look.

"Go!" the moron shouted, and as we dashed toward the water, I said, "He does!" and into the water I went. Peace, quiet, like a fish … not even coming up for a breath. I was at the first buoy, coming up for only a moment. I was back under and on my way to the second platform. I couldn't see Eric, but there was no way he would beat my time. I could hold my breath longer than anyone on my swim team. I was a freak when it came to holding my breath. I used to use it to get my way when I was little. It would always work until they realized it was just something I could do. The only advantage now was in the water. When it was shallow enough to stand, I ran the rest of the way with the waves pushing me until I was almost on the beach. I looked back for Eric Wilson; he was just passing the buoy on his way back.

"Great time, Randolph," he said as I walked past him and lay flat on my back in the sand. "One of the best times we've had."

"Yeah … I'm part fish." I got up and walked back out to wait on Eric, who was walking up out of the water.

"Good job," Eric said.

"You too. I'm sorry," I said.

"Don't be. You were great. Maybe you can teach me how you do that?" he asked as he collapsed on the sand.

"Maybe." I laughed. "Since you're not a Michigan fan."

"Next up … Jones/McGee."

Eric and I joined the rest of the group as, two by two, they swam for the top eight spots who would then compete in the weighted swim for the four shadowing spots. The third and final relay was a forty-yard run and swim with a sandbag that felt like it weighed a hundred pounds. I thought I would die, but I think I got a better time than the rest.

"Okay, guys. Thanks for coming. You all did great, but we only have four spots, so … McGee, Wright, Taylor, and Randolph. Meet here at ten in the morning for pairing assignment. The rest of you, enjoy your week."

Just then the sound of the whistle rang out and, for a moment, startled everyone. "Trouble … straight out!" yelled the guard on the tower. Ben turned and, in an instant, ran toward the water. The rest of us followed, scanning the water for signs of struggle. "Where is he?" someone asked.

"There he is!" someone else said. "Beyond the swells!" By then, a crowd had gathered, looking for a sign of anyone struggling.

Just then I spotted them way out … I mean way out past the buoys that we had just swum to. How did Ben get out that far so quickly? I did not even see him swim out. Did he stay under that long? That was not possible. How? "There they are! He's got him!" someone yelled, and into the water I went, along with several others. I swam out to meet Ben and the man. "How can I help?" I asked as I met them.

"Take his other arm. Flip over on your back, man," he told the man, who was so exhausted he could hardly move. We managed to get him on his back, and I hooked my arm under his armpit and started to swim toward shore.

We were still pretty far out, and the swells were big enough to lose sight of the shoreline, but we just kept swimming, and then four other swimmers were there. "Let me take it," the guy whose last name was McGee said. I was exhausted, so I let him take over.

"You okay, Randolph?" Ben asked.

"I'm okay."

Finally, we were through the swells and could stand. The guy was coughing up salt water but seemed to be okay. "Can you stand?" Ben asked him. The man appeared to be in his fifties or so. He was white as a sheet and could barely

stand or walk, even with the help of Ben and McGee. *Cory,*
I thought.

"I just kept getting farther and farther out. The
swells … I was fighting to get back in, and they just kept
pushing me out. I thought I was going to drown. Thank
you!"

"You have to respect the water … know the current.
Don't ever think you are better than it is." Ben was scold-
ing this man whose life he had probably just saved.

"I will be more careful. I may not get back in the water
any time soon," the man said as we made it out of the
water.

"Just be smart. Call it a day and get some rest."

"I will. Thanks again to all of you," he said. A crowd
had gathered—concerned and curious onlookers.

"That is quite a first day for you guys," Ben said. "See
you tomorrow." I gathered my towel, signed out at the
table, and turned to head back down the beach toward the
beach house.

"Randolph!" I heard him yell. "Pretty impressive for
a princess!" I could feel my face burning … not from the
sun. For a few moments—moments of saving a life, mind
you—I had forgotten he was a moron, and now he had
just reminded me that he was a moron. I did not even look
back. I would not even give him the satisfaction of even
looking at him. *Keep walking. I won't even show up tomorrow.* How could I put up with him all week? Not a chance!
I couldn't walk fast enough. How far was the house any-

way? Finally, I ran up the steps to the house. Once inside, I headed straight for the shower.

"Hey, Luvy, how was your morning? You made the Juniors I'm sure. You can swim like a fish." Aunt Abby was always a cheerleader for me.

"I'm not going back. A man almost drowned. I helped get him to shore … and I'm being stalked by a moron." I headed up the stairs as I heard Aunt Abby saying, "Oh my goodness! What a first day! Is he okay? The drowning man, not the moron! Oh, Luvy, the Carltons decided they are coming over later. They are bringing a guest."

"Great!" I had had enough of people for one day. The hot water from the shower felt so good. I wished it could wash all the things going on in my life away. I wished my family could be together, not moving across the country. If the water could just wash away the events of this day—no drowning man, no feeling of accomplishment, no moron. Maybe it has been a dream. But no, it had not been, and now my plans for the week had changed. Ruined by the *moron*. Sleep … I welcomed it as I lay across my bed. A nap before the Carltons came over … oh joy!

That is why I loved swimming so much—alone in the water, no people, no decisions, just quietness, peacefulness.

I must have slept for hours because the next thing I heard was Aunt Abby calling my name. "Christi! The Carltons are here!"

"Great," I said and then realized how sarcastic it sounded. "I'll be right down." I changed my tone to sound somewhat pleasant. As I threw on some comfy clothes and pulled my hair up in a ponytail, I remembered how much I really liked the Carltons. It would be hard to see Mr. Carlton in a wheelchair. He had loved the beach and the ocean so much. Life has its way of throwing you a curveball. Walking down the stairs, I could hear Mrs. Carlton talking. "He will be staying in the room over the garage for the summer and helping Mr. Carlton with therapy." I could see them sitting in the living area.

"Hey, Luvy. The Carltons have a guest for the summer …" The guy who had been sitting on the sofa with his back to the stairs stood and turned to greet me.

"This is Ben. Ben, this is Christi," Aunt Abby said.

Horrified, I was looking at the moron … Mr. Michigan … the arrogant loser.

"You have got to be kidding me! Are you for real following me? Who are you anyway? THIS CANNOT BE HAPPENING!" I stormed right past all of them onto the porch, letting the screen door slam behind me.

"Christi!" I heard Aunt Abby exclaim.

"It's okay, Mrs. Collins. We've met … not a good first impression on my part, needless to say. I'll try to talk to her." I could hear the moron through the screen door.

Oh no, you won't, I thought and headed off the porch, down the steps, and as I stepped onto the beach, I heard the screen door snap shut.

Chapter Three

"Hey!" I heard him yell. "Wait up!"

Not on your life! I thought as my pace quickened.

"Princess!" he yelled.

Seriously, he did not just call me that again. "My name is not Princess, moron!" I yelled back at him. He was closing the distance between us, so I started to run.

"Okay, I won't call you *princess*, and you don't refer to me as *moron*!" he yelled back.

"No deal, moron, because we are done talking." The only way to drown him out was the water—the quietness of the water. I ran into the waves and dove under ... peace. When I came up for a breath, I was surprised how far out I was and how dark it had gotten. I remembered I was not even supposed to get in the water at night. Aunt Abby was so overprotective. No lifeguards at night. Hardly anyone on the beach at night, but swimming was like walking for me. I was as safe in it at night as in the daytime. Besides, I had to get away from him. It was my only out. I could tread water as long as I had to, to be sure he was gone.

It was dark enough I could not see the shore clearly. Was he still there? Waiting for me to come out? I could not see anyone. Just then I felt something. "Ouch!" I said out loud. Something stung my calf. *Shark!* I thought and started to swim toward the shore. My leg was numb. What if it was a shark? I looked around, trying to stay treading with one leg, and then I saw something—something shining in the water, a glow really—under the surface. Some type of fish that glows?

Suddenly, I could not move. My treading stopped. *Move legs*, I told myself. *Why are my arms not moving?* I sank under the water. *Who's the moron now?* I thought to myself, as my body was frozen and sinking. *Respond, dammit! What is wrong with you? What kind of fish paralyzes you? A stingray? Jellyfish?*

Then I saw it—a perfect ball of light! It was beautiful, like the sun, only under the water. It was circling me like it was watching me. This was no fish, at least none I had ever seen. And then I was being pulled up and through the water. I could not respond. My body would not let me. *Breathe in the water*, my mind was telling me. *Let the water in …* We broke the surface of the water as my lungs gasped for air. He was swimming and holding onto me like I was no weight at all. When we were close enough to shore for him to stand, he carried me and laid me on the shore.

"My leg," I said. "Something hit my leg. I can't feel anything." What he did next—I would have hit him if I could have. He began to suck on my leg, like sucking venom from a snakebite. Maybe that was what it was ... some poisonous sea snake. As he continued the process of extracting whatever it was in my bloodstream, I began to feel my body—first my arms, then my legs. He stood up as if he knew.

"Are you okay?" he asked.

"I think so ..." I felt my leg, expecting to find a cut or gash, but just smooth skin, no scrape. No nothing. "Something bit me. How can there not be a cut or broken skin? Something?" I looked at him, puzzled.

"It was a muscle cramp. You had quite a workout earlier today."

"No. No. No. I saw something in the water glowing, and it hit me. This was not a muscle cramp! And you ... you just sucked something out of my leg! There had to be a wound! How did you do that?"

"Christi. You were about to lose consciousness. All I did was massage a severe muscle cramp. See, no wound, not even a scrape," he said as I looked at him like he was crazy.

"My body may have been unresponsive but not my mind. I know what I saw in the water. And just now! I am not the crazy one."

"If you can walk, let's get back. The tide is coming in. You should stay out of the water at night." He took my arm and helped me to my feet.

"I'm fine," I said and shrugged his hand away. And actually I was. It was as if nothing had happened. My leg was fine. But something had happened. I was not hallucinating or dreaming. Something was in the water, and something had happened to me, and for some reason, Ben did not want me to question it. We did not speak walking back to Aunt Abby's, and as I started up the steps, he did not follow me. "Ben," I turned and called to him. "Thanks for whatever you did for me."

"It's what I'm trained to do. Say good night to your aunt, and tell the Carltons I'm calling it a day. See you in the morning," he said and turned toward the Carltons' beachfront home.

I sat down on the glider on the porch. What a day! So much for relaxing at the beach! *I can't tell Aunt Abby. She will freak ... not want me to go in the water at all. Maybe it was a cramp. Maybe I was blacking out when I saw the light ... maybe.*

"Luvy," Aunt Abby said as she came out the screen door. "How long have you been sitting here?"

"Not long," I said. "Come sit with me. Are the Carltons still here?"

"No. Mr. Carlton did not feel well, so they went back early. Where were you? It has been hours. I was getting worried."

"Hours? What time is it?"

"Oh, ten o'clock or so. I figured you and Ben were talking. Seems like a nice young man, don't you think?" she asked.

"Remember at the airport, that guy ran into me and I dumped my tray?"

Aunt Abby just sat and stared at me.

"It was Ben, and now he is here. Lead lifeguard and living next door with the Carltons. Don't you think that is so weird?" I asked her, expecting her to find it all as bizarre as I did.

"It is a small world, Luvy, and once you get to know Ben, you may not find it so weird," she explained. "He may feel it is as odd as you do. Don't read too much into it, Luvy. Have fun! You are only here for a week. Make the most of it. He loves the water as much as you do. He is doing water therapy with Mr. Carlton. They adore him. Maybe you should keep an open mind."

Part of me wanted to tell her what had just happened, but I was fine. I could not even explain to her what had happened because I did not even know. "You left your phone on the counter," she said as she handed it to me. "Your mom and dad both called. Why don't you give them a call before you come in?" Aunt Abby kissed my forehead, took one last look at the white foam waves lapping on the beach, took a deep breath, and turned to go inside. "Goodnight, Luvy. Love you."

"To the moon and back," I said to her as the screen door closed.

"Hi, Dad!"

"Hey, how's my girl? Having fun being with Abby?"

"Aunt Abby's great. The beach is great. I miss you, Dad. I miss my friends." I suddenly felt homesick.

"Honey, your week will fly by. I'm surprised you have not already made some new friends."

"No friends here, Dad."

"You will change your mind. When I talk to you by the middle of the week, you will not want to come home."

"If you say so," I said. "I'll call you tomorrow. Love you, Dad."

"Love you," he said as I ended the call.

My mom. I thought about the conversation we would have. I so did not want to talk about moving out there. Not tonight. I hit Call. "This is Joni. Leave a message." Thank God, voicemail! "Hey, Mom! I'm fine. Having a great time. Talk to you soon! Love you!" Glad that conversation would take place another day. I couldn't think about anything else today. I was going to bed.

As I turned to latch the screen door behind me, something caught my eye out in the water … a light. Not just one light but several, at least a dozen. Night divers? I'd never seen that here. I blinked to focus my eyes. No tricks of light from the moon. There were lights. One. Two. Three. Four. Ten of them in a line about forty yards offshore. I was certain one of them was the one I saw in the water, the one that had hit me. "What are you?" I asked out loud. And then they were gone. I blinked. Nothing. No sign of anything. Just darkness and whitecaps. *Oh, Christi! Maybe you are losing it!* I locked the doors and turned off the light and headed upstairs for bed. I usually left my window open so I could hear the water. Tonight I thought I would close it. It was a little chilly.

It seemed I just closed my eyes when my alarm went off. Every morning at the beach, Aunt Abby and I get out early. She looks for shells and gets her walk in. I run. You can run for two miles on sand packed down like bricks with only a few people out that early. It's my favorite part of the day. Aunt Abby was dressed and on the porch waiting for me. "I'm ready," I said as I popped out the door.

"Coffee?"

"No, I'm good 'til we get back," I replied. And we headed to the beach. "Catch you on the way back!" I said as I started to jog away.

"Be careful," Aunt Abby said.

Running was my next favorite thing to swimming. Again, I could do it alone, in my own world. But here I had both, and even when I ran, I could enjoy the ocean and I almost always saw dolphins.

This time each year they are here … swimming each morning just offshore, swimming laps with their babies. Sometimes I pretend they see me and are racing me as I run. It was odd they were not surfacing. I decided to stop and look for them. Nothing. *Hmmm, sleeping in I guess,* I thought and concentrated on my running. *How can I explain away last night?* My thoughts were not on running. He, the moron, had sucked something out of my leg. I'm sorry—I could not have imagined that, could I? Oh my God! I didn't remember him spitting it out. Wasn't that how it was done in the movies? You sucked it out then spit it out. He did not spit! How could he have done that? I had to have imagined it. Too many movies I guess. *But the lights … stop it … I am making myself crazy.* The adrenaline of the whole day had been too much, I was sure. After all, I was running … leg as good as ever. *Where are the dolphins?* I always ran to the pier, about a mile and a half and then back. It was good exercise to start the day.

Not too many people fishing off the pier today. Good for the fishes, I thought as I turned to make my trek back. A few more early risers had made their way out by then, so I had to weave my way up and down, dodging bikes and people running their dogs. I could tell it was Mrs. Jackson from behind—long flowing shirt, big floppy hat—and I had been exchanging pleasantries with Mrs. Jackson for years on my morning runs. Mrs. Jackson and Sam. I scanned the water for Sam. Chasing his stick no doubt. Didn't see him. "Hey, Mrs. Jackson! How are you? Where is Sam?" I had always taken the time to talk to and play awhile with Sam. I love dogs—cats too, but dogs love to run and swim just like me.

"Hey, Christi! Look at you … all grown up!" she said as she stopped to chat with me.

"Where is Sam?" I asked again as I looked around, expecting him to knock me down at any moment. Sam is a golden retriever with a personality that was friendly with everyone. Her face saddened as she said to me that she had lost Sam.

"I'm so sorry. When? He was young and healthy. What happened?" I asked, not sure I should have asked her to recount her loss.

"Here, just a week ago. We were walking, our night-time walk. He was fine, and we were throwing and fetching in the water. You know how he loved that. I threw it a little farther out because he loves to swim. You saw him swim, Christi—he was a good swimmer. He went out, and … he did not come back in. I called him. I looked for him … I never found him." She began to cry.

"Oh! I'm so sorry. What do you mean? His body never washed up?"

"No, no one found him. He was just there, and then he was gone." I hugged her as she relived her loss. Running would not be the same without seeing Sam. I tried to comfort her, feeling her pain. "In time, maybe you can adopt another dog," I said, asking a question more than making a statement.

"Maybe," she responded. "How's Abby?"

"Great! Our week is already flying by. Gotta run! See you in the morning, Mrs. Jackson."

"Enjoy your week, Christi! Tell your aunt hello for me."

"I will," I said as I jogged away, leaving her looking out into the water as if Sam would come swimming to her any moment.

Sad. Where are the dolphins today? I asked myself again. I had never been here this week and not seen them in the morning. So strange. A lot of things recently had seemed strange. Aunt Abby had said I had been gone for hours last night. How could that be? I had walked down the beach, swam out, and something happened. The next thing I remember, *he* was doing something to my leg. That could not have been hours, even though spending a minute in his presence seemed like hours. I laughed to myself. I guess I should be glad he was there. I may have been like Sam.

Oh my God! What if that is what happened to Sam? Something in the water got Sam too! Now I really had seen too many movies. Besides, his body would have come ashore. *Wouldn't it?* I asked myself. Just then, I saw something in the water. Or did I? I stopped and looked into the waves. There! Something large … I lost it again. I started to wade into the water, straining to see it again as the tide seemed to move whatever it was … then I felt something wash against my shin. I screamed. As I stepped back, a pelican washed by me onto the sand and stuck into a mote of half-washed-out sand castle.

Seriously, I thought to myself. *Get a grip. It's just a bird. What should I do with him?* I asked myself. "Stay right here!" I said to the dead bird. I would bring a shovel and bag from Aunt Abby's and bury it. I was only a few minutes up the beach from the house. Maybe I could get back before some kids found it.

I could see Aunt Abby standing by the water with Mrs. Carlton as I approached. "Do we have a shovel?" I asked as I stopped beside them. "Hi, Mrs. Carlton."

"Just plastic sand shovels. Why?" Aunt Abby asked.

"There's a dead pelican down the beach." I pointed in the direction I had just jogged from. "I want to get it before some kid comes upon it. It is not a pretty sight." As I explained, I could see Mr. Carlton in the water. Ben was holding him in a chair position, and Mr. Carlton was moving his arms across the water. "You're doing great," I heard Ben say. "I think that's enough for today."

"Maybe tomorrow we can go a little farther out?" Mr. Carlton asked as Ben picked him up and carried him toward the three of us who were still standing at the water's edge.

"We would need help for that," Ben said as he neared where we stood. "Maybe the junior lifeguard would want to help us tomorrow with your therapy session," Ben said, stopping in front of us, holding Mr. Carlton in his arms.

All four of them were looking at me, waiting for me to respond. "Of course, Mr. Carlton," I said, glaring at the moron. "I would love to help you." I turned to Mr. Carlton. "I'll see you in the morning." I touched Mr. Carlton's arm as I turned to run up toward the house. "Gotta get the pelican," I said.

"Shovel and pails are in the storage area in the garage!" Aunt Abby called to me.

"Okay!" I yelled back. I took two plastic sand shovels and a garbage bag from the garage and headed back down the beach to where the dead bird had washed up. Good. It was still there. No kids had found it. I opened the bag and scooped it up with both shovels and put it into the plastic bag. What graceful birds they were. Gliding along the water and the gulls … strange … where were the birds?

I looked around—on the beach, in the air—silence. Not a gull, not a sandpiper, not a seabird of any kind. "How weird is that?" I said out loud.

"What?" I heard him say. "How weird is it that a princess would be playing near a sand castle?"

I felt my face turning red again as I turned to face the moron and give him a piece of my mind once and for all.

Chapter Four

"I'm sorry," he said as I whirled around with the plastic shovels in my hand ready to clobber him. "I won't call you that again."

"You don't even know me!" I yelled at him.

"I found your bracelet, and I saved your life," he stated, just like he did those things routinely and he was justified in his actions.

"I didn't ask you for either of those things, and why are you standing here right now?" I looked at him with a "drop dead and I will bury you with this bird" look.

"I came to help you with the pelican," he said as I saw he had a real shovel in his hand.

"I can manage," I said as I picked up the bag and started down the beach.

"Are you going to dig with those plastic shovels?" he asked as he walked behind me.

"If I have to!" I yelled back at him.

"Well, you don't have to. It's the least I can do. We don't have to talk. I'll just dig the hole."

I did not respond. I just quickened my pace down the beach to the protected dunes that separated the beach from the marsh. I could bury it there. Crazy, I know, but I've always buried the animals I've found. Squirrels. Birds. Even fish. Ever since I was little. They are all God's creation, and they deserve the dignity of a burial.

We didn't speak as we walked. He stayed behind me and waited until I chose the perfect spot to bury the pelican. "Here," I said and stepped aside as he dug a hole big enough for the huge bird. He stepped aside as I placed the bag into the hole, gently tucking in the sides of the plastic bag. I used one of the shovels I had and, along with Ben, covered the dead pelican and smoothed out the sand so you could hardly tell it had been disturbed. I stood and stared at the grave of this graceful bird.

"May the ocean's gentle breeze fill your wings to flight and sail you safely home," he said and then turned to walk back to the beach. I turned and followed him down the beach. We did not speak nor did he turn to look back at me. How could a moron say something so sweet? He must be better with animals than with people. But then I remembered how gentle he had been with Mr. Carlton this morning, just a few minutes earlier in fact. Maybe I had been too hard on him. Maybe I had been the moron. *Not!* An apology and a couple of moments of humility didn't excuse him.

As I turned to the steps leading up to the beach house, he was walking up the steps of the Carltons. Without turning my head, I strained my eyes in his direction to see if he was looking toward me. He was not. *Good*, I thought. *I don't want him looking at me anyway.* But why was I looking at him?

Aunt Abby had breakfast waiting when I walked in. Cereal and fresh fruit was on the table. "Better eat quick," she said as I glanced at the clock. 9:50 a.m. I practically drank my Rice Chex and then threw on my suit, grabbed a banana, kissed Aunt Abby, and ran out the door. Our sessions started at 10:00. It was a fifteen-minute walk to the guard station, so I would have to run. Didn't want to be late the first day. Everyone was already there as I jogged up to the lifeguard station.

"Good morning, everyone," Ben said as he addressed the shadow guards and the other three lifeguards. "We will pair up this morning for the week. We will man the stands, and the junior with me will patrol the beach today. Then we will alternate stations for the rest of the week," he said as he led the brief meeting.

"We are each assigned a number and will draw to pair up," he continued as he placed numbers 1 through 4 in two cups and began to draw numbers out. I had been assigned the number 1 since my time on the relays were the best. The pairings were made: number 3 junior with number 2 guard, number 2 junior with number 4 guard, number 4 junior with number 3 guard, which left me—number 1 junior with number 1 guard. As luck would have it, of course, Ben was number 1 guard, being the lead. Could this week get any worse?

"Okay, guys. Head out. Back here at three o'clock," Ben said as the guards and their shadows headed to their assigned stands. "Ready, Randolph?" he asked, and without waiting for me to answer, he headed down the beach toward the dock.

"What do we do when we patrol?" I asked him, reluctant to start a conversation with him.

"Watch the water. Listen for panic screams, and know the difference from having-fun screams. Hope we don't have a demonstration of them. Say hello to Mrs. Jackson," he continued as he walked over to Mrs. Jackson as she stood where I had left her earlier this morning. "Good morning, Mrs. Jackson. Beautiful sunrise, wasn't it?" he said as he stood beside her and looked out across the water.

"Yes, it was, Ben," she replied.

"You know that pup is still available. They have not found a home yet."

I listened as he talked to Mrs. Jackson, and she hung her head.

"It's okay if you're not ready. When you are, there is a friend waiting for you." He put his arm around her shoulder and just stood beside her for a couple of minutes. Looking, just looking at the water with her.

I didn't say anything. I couldn't. Suddenly there was a lump in my throat. I could hardly swallow. Then he turned and again started down the beach, and I fell in beside him. "Does she stand there all day?" I asked him.

"Most of the day, yes," he said. "Gives her comfort, I guess."

As we walked along the beach, we occasionally stopped and talked to tourists. Stopped to help three kids who were building a sand castle (without any princess comments).

"I want to be a lifeguard when I get older," one of the little boys said.

"Me too!" the others chimed in.

"Study hard. Get good grades. Take swim lessons, and before you know it, you can shadow, just like Christi here," he said as he looked at me and smiled.

"Yeah ... before you know it. I used to build sand castles right here on this very beach, and look at me now ... I'm shadowing with the lead lifeguard," I said with pride. *Did I just say that?* I thought to myself. Must be the sun affecting the brain because it sounded like I was giving credit to Ben. Well, I guess he was the lead guard and I was the most qualified shadower. So we were the best team on the beach, as far as a lifeguard team was concerned, I mean.

As we started up the steps to the pier, people were coming down, gear packed up and heading out. "Giving up so soon?" Ben asked. "Yep. Kept snapping my line." We walked on down the pier as everyone was packing up. "What's up, George?" Ben asked as we approached a man in the middle of the pier, also packing away his bait and tackle for the day.

"Turtles, I guess," the man said. "Something keeps snapping the lines. Haven't seen anything, but something is out there. I mean everybody's lines are snapped. Never seen anything like it."

"Yeah," Ben said. "Maybe a nest of sea turtles. Better luck tomorrow."

"I hope so," the man named George said as he picked up his gear. "New friend?" he asked Ben.

"Yeah, this is Christi. She is patrolling with me today."

"Hey, young lady," He wiped his hand on his pants and held out his hand.

"Nice to meet you," I said as I shook his hand.

"You are with a good guy, missy. You enjoy your week."

I smiled pleasantly as he walked away. "See ya, George," Ben called to him and walked to the end of the pier and looked out at the vastness of the ocean before us.

"How long have you been guarding here?" I asked him. "Everyone knows you."

"A long time," he answered. "Not guarding but coming to this beach for a long time. Just like you."

"How did you meet the Carltons?" I was suddenly curious about this guy I was shadowing.

"I'm studying to be a physical therapist. Sports medicine with water therapy. Mr. Carlton was one of my intern patients. They hired me for the summer since I come here anyway. It worked out for both of us."

"Do your parents live in Michigan?" I asked.

"My parents are not here," he answered, still looking out over the water as if he was expecting to see something.

"Where are they?" I continued. "I know they are not here. Do they live in Michigan?"

"For someone who did not want to talk to me, you sure ask a lot of questions," he said as his eyes turned to me.

"Just trying to understand."

"Hmmm," he mumbled and turned back down the pier. I followed, and suddenly everything seemed so weirdly … not normal.

"Where are the gulls?" I asked.

We both stopped and looked around the pier, normally filled with people fishing and gulls hoping for a worm or a small fish thrown their way. It was just Ben and I. No people, but even more odd, no birds. No birds anywhere.

"Maybe a storm's coming in. They can sense it long before we do." He tried to explain it, but I could not let it go.

"Ben, this is just too weird. Have you ever *not* seen gulls on the pier, storm or no storm?" He did not answer me. "Have you?" I persisted.

"Why do birds do what they do? I can't answer that. It's the fish and bait that draws them. No fish today."

"It's more than that. I feel something is not right. Everything feels weird."

"Weird?" He suddenly seemed upset. "If anything has been weird, it's you. You don't want to talk, and now you expect me to know what birds are thinking? We need to finish our patrol," he said and left me standing there looking at him.

I looked around the pier again and then followed Ben off the pier. We finished our patrol not saying much to each other, stopping to have small talk to people along the way. I mostly picked up trash left from tourists oblivious to littering on the beach. Everyone was enjoying their day in the sun, splashing in the waves, not noticing anything out of the ordinary. Off in the distance, there was a flash of lightning.

"See, a storm's coming in," he said as he took out his radio and paged the guard station. "Lightning. Let's clear the water," he said into the radio.

I blew the whistle I had been given at check-in. "Out of the water, please!" I yelled as tourists waded out of the water, disappointed that their day was cut short. The lightning was more frequent now, and people were hurrying to pack up and scurry off before the rain came. And it was coming. Fast. The clouds were rolling in, and as the last of the stragglers got off the beach, it let loose. We looked to make certain everyone was out of the water and off the beach. And then we ran to the shelter closest to that part of the beach.

"Oh my gosh!" I exclaimed. We were soaked. "Where did that come from?"

"We can't predict nature or the weather," Ben said. "Nothing we can do about it, so don't worry about it."

"Kinda like Ohio State dominating Michigan in football … nothing you can do about it, so no need to worry." There was a long silence, and then he burst into laughter and so did I. I laughed so hard my side hurt. It felt good though.

"So why are you here with your aunt?" he asked me when the laughter began to subside. "Where is the rest of your family?"

"Oh, it would take me all week to explain my family," I said.

"We have all week," he said with a sincerity in his voice that almost made me open up to him.

"Thought you were majoring in physical therapy, not psychology. The rain is slacking. Are we going back?" I stood and started back toward the beach.

"It's almost three o'clock. Go home. I'll check in with the others. See you in the morning," he said as he walked past me to the entrance of the beach.

I turned and headed toward the beach house, walking along the road that ran parallel to the beach. It was just a couple of blocks to the house. It was still raining, and occasionally, there was a rumble of thunder. *No more beach time today, I'm afraid*, I thought as I headed up the stairs to the house. *Pretty smart birds.*

"Are you drenched, Luvy?" Aunt Abby called as she heard the door close.

"Yes, I'm soaked and freezing. I'm going to jump in the shower, then I'll be right down."

"Do you want to eat in or not?" she asked.

"Let's just hang out. Eat something here," I said.

"Sounds great to me. We'll come up with something," Aunt Abby said. "I laid fresh towels out for you."

"Thanks, I'll be down in a few," I called as I headed up the stairs. I decided to draw water for a bath instead. As I soaked, my thoughts wandered to Ben. He wasn't so bad … not nearly the moron I thought he was. I smiled to myself as I contemplated the thought. *And he is cute too*, I said to myself as my head slipped under the water. *What if we had met differently? He told George I was his friend. Could we be friends? Girlfriend and boyfriend?* I burst up out of the water. That was only two minutes tops … now he was ruining my time.

"Ugh," I said out loud as I got out of the tub, dried off, and dressed to go down to dinner with Aunt Abby. We had not talked much yet. The whole evening together … it would be nice. I could smell the pepperoni as I came down the stairs. We always ordered pizza at least once while we were here.

"I talked to your mom today," Aunt Abby said as I grabbed a slice and a Coke and headed for the couch.

"How's things in the Wild West?" I asked as I reached for the remote.

"She's anxious for you to come out. She is planning on it."

"She's going to be disappointed," I said as I snuggled up under a comfy throw. It was still raining and beginning to get dark out. Lightning would light up the sky with a crash of thunder soon following.

"Change is always hard, Luvy. It's hard for your mom too …" I could hear her, but the news on the TV had caught my attention. As I grabbed the remote for the volume, the reporter was set up on the beach just north of us. Recorded earlier, "Fish are washing up, and dead birds are being found up and down the beach." She was speaking into the camera and turning to look out at the water. She continued, "Is this a weird phenomenon of nature, or is something happening with the water? Angela O'Bryan reporting from Garden City Beach."

"Have you seen the news?" I asked as I changed the channel to see if anyone else was reporting anything.

"No. What is it?"

"I don't know. It feels like something is going on."

"What do you mean?" Aunt Abby asked.

"Dead fish. Dead birds. I've seen lights in the water, Aunt Abby."

"There are always ships and barges offshore …"

"No, not on the water—in the water," I continued. "And they were too close to be scuba divers. No classes even going on … and especially not at night."

"Hmmm … I'm sure there will be an explanation for all of it. What did the report say?" she asked me as I was still searching for another report.

"Just caught the end, nothing really."

"Maybe the storm has something to do with it," she said.

"Maybe …" I mused as a flash of lightning lit up the whole sky. A crash of thunder and then silence and darkness. The power was off.

"Great. I'll get candles," Aunt Abby said. "Pizza by candlelight. That will be fun. Do you think you should call your mom, Luvy?" she said as we lit the candles she had brought with her from the kitchen.

"Maybe tomorrow. I think I'll go to bed early. I'm helping Ben with Mr. Carlton in the morning, so I want to get my run in first. I'll be up early. Besides, talking will not do any good. I'm not changing my mind."

"She just wants to hear from you. Be sure to call her tomorrow. She'll get worried."

"She knows I'm fine. I'm with you." Aunt Abby just gave me that look. "Okay, I'll call her tomorrow."

"I think I'll turn in as well," Aunt Abby said as I cleared the pizza and drinks.

"Yeah, not much else to do. Good night, Aunt Abby."

"Right behind you, Luvy. Good night. It will be better tomorrow," she said.

"Promise?" I asked. Aunt Abby just laughed and started up the stairs behind me.

The rain was pounding the glass of my window in my room. Wow! I thought as I pressed my nose against the pane. "There in the water—lights. Oh my gosh … where are my binoculars? Stay there!" I said out loud, talking to these … these lights, as if they would hear me. I threw open my closet and frantically searched for my binoculars. Good! They were there!

As I ran back to the window, I tried to focus through the lenses. Yes, they were there—lots of lights under the water. I watched for at least a minute, straining to make sense of whatever it was I was seeing. Was there someone in the water? Yes, someone was coming out of the water!

Then the lights were gone. I looked side to side. They were gone. I focused on the figure coming out of the water. Did they not see the lights? Did they not know it was storming? What were they doing in the water?

I could now see the person walking up out of the waves and onto the beach. It was Ben. A flash of lightning lit up the sky, and as I was looking at Ben through the scope, he stopped and looked straight at me. Eye to eye through the lens. I whirled away from the window and pinned my back to the wall. My heart pounded. Why was Ben in the water? Did he see me? What did he have to do with the lights? Thunder shook the house as the power came on.

Chapter Five

The dreams came like waves. I was in the water; my legs felt like weights were tied to them. I was sinking. My lungs felt like they were going to burst, and there was a light all around me. Like it was drawing me into it. Each time, I would tell myself to let the water and the light in. Suddenly I would be at the surface, gasping for air, and then I would sink all over again. The same thing over and over. Why couldn't I just wake up? Somehow I knew I was dreaming, but I just couldn't make myself wake up.

Again I was under the water ... this time, I couldn't fight it. I would not fight it. Let the light have me. Then I heard a siren. Help was coming. It was louder. I awoke to my alarm clock ringing by my bed. *Thank God!* I thought and wished I could pull the covers back over my head.

It seemed so real because of what I had just experienced a couple of nights ago. Ben had pulled me out. Ben ...

should I question him about last night? He knew I saw him. What possible explanation could he have about the lights? It was not my imagination. I would confront him this morning after our session with Mr. Carlton. Should people even be in the water? Had anyone else see the lights? Questions that needed answers. But now, I needed to stick to my routine and take my morning run.

The house was still quiet as I went downstairs. Aunt Abby was still sleeping. I grabbed a jacket and slipped out the door, trying to not wake her. The smell of fish was so thick in the air it made me gasp out loud. The storm must have really churned up the shells, but wow, this was awful. The sun was just beginning to rise over the water as I stepped onto the beach. I froze as I looked down the beach for as far as I could see, there were dead fish. Everywhere. Left on the sand from the tide that was going out. The stench was overwhelming. It made me cover my mouth and nose. I thought I was going to throw up!

"Oh my gosh!" I said out loud. Other people were venturing out onto the beach, looking in amazement at what had happened in the aftermath of the storm. "Aunt Abby!" I screamed as I ran back into the house, letting the screen door slam as I flew up the stairs. "Aunt Abby!" I called again as I pounded on her door.

"What is it, Luvy?" she said as she opened the bedroom door. "Are you okay?"

"You have to see this!" was all I could say as I dragged her down the stairs and out onto the porch.

"Oh my!" she said as she covered her mouth and nose with her hands, the smell also hitting her before she saw the cause of it. "Good Lord in heaven," she whispered as the sea of dead fish, big and small, glistened like shiny rocks as the sun rose over the water. "What's happened?" she asked out loud.

"Could the storm have done this?" I asked her. "Some kind of electrical energy in the water?" My mind tried to rationalize it all. But how could Ben withstand that?

"I don't know," Aunt Abby said. "Let's turn on the news. I have to call John. He will be hearing about this … the whole country will." She started back into the house.

"I'll be in," I said to her.

"Don't go near the water, Christi," she said to me.

"I know. I won't." I walked back out onto the beach. The water was so beautiful and peaceful. Just like any other day. But what was happening? Down the beach, I could see Mrs. Jackson kneeling by the water's edge. Big floppy hat. Definitely Mrs. Jackson! I took off in a sprint, dodging dead fish and people who were looking on in awe of this gruesome sight. Mrs. Jackson was sobbing as I ran to her and knelt beside her. There in front of her was a carcass. The carcass of what appeared to be a dog. In amongst all the dead fish, the partial remains of Sam. I knelt beside her and put my arms around her.

"I've been praying for this," she said. "I wanted him to come back to me so I could bury him. I prayed for this. This is my fault."

"Oh no, Mrs. Jackson." I tried to comfort her. "God wouldn't do this. There is an explanation. Let me go get a shovel, and I'll help you with Sam. I'll be right back." I turned and ran back down the beach, dodging more curious onlookers this time.

A news crew was beginning to set up for a live report. Same ones I had seen on TV the night before, I think. As I passed the Carltons, I thought of Mr. Carlton. No therapy today. Too bad, he had been looking forward to it. As I glanced up at their house, I could see the curtain pulled aside in the garage apartment. Ben was standing looking out. Looking at me. I looked at him, looked back down the beach, turned, and ran up the steps into the house.

"Shoot," I said. "We don't have a shovel." Remember the pelican? Aunt Abby was on the phone and glued to the TV, waiting for a newsbreak. "Have to borrow the Carlton's shovel," I said as I headed back out.

"Don't mess with the fish," Aunt Abby said. "We don't know," she added.

"It's Mrs. Jackson's dog, Sam."

"Don't touch anything," I heard her say as the screen door shut behind me.

"I won't!" I yelled back to her. I pounded on the door of the Carltons. Nancy Carlton opened the door, and I stepped inside. "Can I borrow your shovel, Mrs. Carlton? Aunt Abby doesn't have one. It's Sam." I saw Mr. Carlton in their living room looking out onto the beach. He was standing! No wheelchair! No walker! Standing on his own! I looked at him and then at Mrs. Carlton. I couldn't speak.

"It's a miracle," she said. Mr. Carlton did not even turn around. He was just staring out at the water. "He just got up this morning and walked downstairs. Hasn't said a word yet. He jHHjjjjjjjjust stares out the window. The shovel is in the garage. Of course you can use it. You can't bury all the fish though." She half smiled with tears in her eyes.

"Thanks, Mrs. Carlton. I'm so happy for you, Mr. Carlton," I said to him. He seemed to not even know I was there.

"The utility door is unlocked. The shovel is inside."

"I'll bring it right back," I said as I closed the door and headed down the steps to the door of the storage room under their garage. The shovel was just inside the door. I looked for a box. I found a tote that had a bunch of beach toys inside. I dumped them out and took the tote. Aunt Abby would replace it. With the tote and shovel in hand, I headed down the beach toward where I had left Mrs. Jackson. I saw her walking toward me as I got closer to her, with … Ben. He was carrying a box.

"I tried to hurry," I said to Mrs. Jackson as I approached.

"We had to move him before they got here," she said.

"They?" I asked.

"The authorities," he answered for her. "They will be here any minute. We have to hurry," he continued as we hurriedly headed down the beach to the dunes.

I suddenly felt sick again. I had buried all my pet gold-fish. The thought of hundreds of dead fish brought tears to my eyes. Mrs. Jackson picked a spot near the marsh near where we had buried the pelican. Ben and I quickly dug a hole, and she placed Sam into the grave and began to sob as we covered the box with the sand we had just removed. She gently smoothed the sand and wrote the words "Faithful Friend and Companion" in the sand.

"Thank you," she said to Ben and me.

"I have to get back. I need to check in with Beach Patrol," Ben said. "Will you help Mrs. Jackson back?"

"Yes, but I need to talk to you," I responded.

"Not now. I have to go." He looked at me with a sad-ness in his eyes. That same sadness came over me, and my eyes filled with tears. "It's going to be okay," he said as he turned away and ran back down the beach.

It didn't feel like it was going to be okay … never okay again.

I waited as Mrs. Jackson said her good-byes to Sam. I had left her alone and stood by the marsh. From here above the beach looking at the water, it was beautiful. Except when the breeze caught the smell, it seemed like any other day.

"Thanks, honey," Mrs. Jackson said as she walked up behind me.

"It's the least we could do for Sam," I said to her as we headed back up the beach.

"You and Ben are good kids," she said.

"How long have you known Ben?" I asked her, seizing the opportunity to learn more about him.

"Oh, since he was little. The whole family came here for years on vacation. They would rent the Wilsons' beach house, right next door to me. Tragic what happened," she continued.

"What happened?" I asked her as walked along.

"Oh, honey, people still talk about the boating accident."

"Accident?" I looked at her.

"It was just a couple of years ago. A fishing trip, the whole family … Jason, Jennifer, Lisa, and Ben. Ben was the only one they found."

"What? Oh my God, what happened?"

"He was in shock. He remembered a storm came up, the boat capsized. Ben is such a strong swimmer. They found him the next day. Never found anyone else. He is such a lovely boy. He understood about Sam … he knew my pain."

"His whole family drowned?" I couldn't wrap my mind around what she was telling me.

"The whole family and the crew of the fishing charter … just Ben survived."

"Does he have any other family?" I continued to ask questions.

"Not that I know or remember. Went right off to college after that—the only way he got through it, I guess."

"Wow!" was my only response. Did Aunt Abby know what happened? I'm sure the Carltons would have known.

"How can you go on after something like that?" I thought out loud.

"He is a strong boy," Mrs. Jackson replied. "With a sweet spirit despite what he has been through."

I felt bad for the way I had treated him. But he would still have to answer to the weird things I had seen that he was involved in. And the lights? Maybe it was a dive team … searching for his family's remains? But at night? No. He would have to have a different explanation than that.

"Oh my God," I said out loud. "We've been in the water all week … what if?" The loudspeaker overpowered my thoughts and drowned out my words.

"Clear the beach," he was saying. "Please check in at one of the tents being set up at the beach entrances. Clear the beach please. Check with the authorities at one of the tents at the beach entrance," he repeated.

The authorities had already arrived? That was quick. The news coverage from last night must have gotten attention. There were people in, like, hazmat suits collecting the dead fish from the beach and in the water, collecting vials of ocean water.

"I'd better check with Aunt Abby," I told Mrs. Jackson.

"Yes, you had better. Thanks again … for Sam," she said as I hugged her and ran up the steps into the beach house. Aunt Abby was sitting at the dining room table with Mrs. Carlton.

"I can't leave without him, and he refuses to go," she was saying to Aunt Abby.

"Christy!" Aunt Abby said as I entered the room.

"Are you guys leaving, Mrs. Carlton?" I asked her, wondering if that meant Ben would leave too.

"As soon as we are cleared. We all are, Luvy," Aunt Abby answered for her. "We don't know what chemical might be in the water the CDC and EPA are testing. They want to check all residents before we leave the area."

"They think we are contaminated?" I asked.

"They just want to be cautious. As soon as they can, we will be checked, and just to be safe, we are asked to leave the area. We will head home," Abby continued.

"I won't leave him," Mrs. Carlton said. "It's a miracle! He can walk, Abby! Like nothing ever happened, but he just stands there, looking at the water. When I talk to him about leaving, all he says is 'This is our home. I'm not leaving.' I'm afraid to stay if they are warning us to leave. What can I do though? Can they make you leave if you choose to stay?" she asked.

"I don't know." Aunt Abby put her hand on her shoulder. "He'll make the right decision. Let's see what the authorities say. The notice said as soon as they can get to us, so let's hope it's soon." Abby walked her to the door. "It's so great for Bob. It's going to be fine." She hugged Mrs. Carlton.

"Why doesn't it feel like it?" she asked as she walked out and Aunt Abby closed the door behind her.

"It may be tomorrow, Luvy, but as soon as we are cleared, we are heading home. I'm going to start packing things up."

"What if it's nothing dangerous, just some weird thing with the fish?" I asked.

"Uncle John wants us home. I talked with your mom and dad, and they are worried too. We can always come back once things are normal," she said and headed upstairs. "I'm going to get started packing."

Normal … I thought. This trip had been a far cry from normal, that was for sure. I turned and walked out onto the porch. It was so quiet—no kids screaming having fun, no loud voices, not even from the loudspeaker blasting warnings. And no gulls squawking their presence. The birds knew to leave before we did. Smart birds.

The four-wheeler stopped in front of the Carltons', and Ben got off, said something to the other patrol officers, and turned toward the house as they drove off down the beach.

"Hey!" I yelled and ran down the stairs across the dunes to the steps of the Carltons.

"Not supposed to be on the beach, princess," he said as he stopped in front of me.

"I'm not on the beach, and you said you would not call me that. Besides, you shouldn't be on the beach or in the water. What were you doing in the water last night? You know I saw you. What are the lights, Ben? I saw you … coming out of the water." I looked at him, expecting an answer.

"You don't know what you saw," he said as he stepped around me toward the house.

"Maybe the authorities would be interested in your water activities at night."

He stopped, turned to me, and said, "You don't want to do that."

"Why, Ben? Why wouldn't I want to do that? What are you doing out there? Is that what is killing the fish? Some kind of weird experiment or what? What are the lights, Ben?"

He just looked at me. "Meet me at the dunes tonight. Ten o'clock," he said as he turned to go into the house.

"Now, Ben! Tell me now!" I yelled at him.

"Tonight. Ten o'clock." He closed the door behind him.

It would have to wait. But what if we had to leave before that? I would let them know what I had seen. I could not just pretend I had not seen anything. If we were here overnight, I would have to sneak out. Aunt Abby would not want me out on the dunes. I would have to. I had to know. Tonight ... 10:00.

Chapter Six

Aunt Abby had put all the clothes we had worn in a plastic bag and had packed most of the rest. We spent most of the day putting things away, bringing in chairs. I always hated this part because it meant our week was over, and now it was being cut short. I called my mom and dad to assure them that I was fine. My mom tried to use it to her advantage, trying to persuade me those things never happen in Wyoming. Nice try. We watched the news to hear them verify that we were being quarantined until the possibility of contamination was eliminated.

The evening passed, and no one knocked on our door. My plan was to go to bed early and try to convince Aunt Abby to do the same. I felt bad that I would go out later without her permission, but she would never let me go out by the water. Maybe I should have insisted he talk then or meet me here. After all, Aunt Abby should hear what he had to say. I could not tell her, and I had to find out what he had to say. If he wanted to hurt me, he would not have saved me. I had seen the side of him that Mrs. Jackson had seen. Whatever he had to say, whatever he was involved in, he would not hurt or endanger me. I didn't think …

Aunt Abby was still up. She was glued to the news for any updates the news breaks would bring. It was ten o'clock. Darn. I had to go. I threw the escape ladder out the window and fixed the pillows under the covers so that if Aunt Abby checked on me, she hopefully would not come in.

I opened the bedroom door and yelled, "Good night, Aunt Abby!"

"Good night, Luvy! I'll be up in a while."

I closed my bedroom door, climbed out the window, closed it as much as I could, and started down the rope ladder. I dropped onto the ground by the porch. I could hear the TV still on. I moved over the dunes between the house and the beach, trying to avoid the light from the house. Then it was a sprint to the marsh. I stayed as close to the dunes lining the beach front houses as I could, afraid patrols may be close to the water. They would, for sure, escort me home if I was caught out. Aunt Abby would not be happy.

Don't leave. Don't leave, I kept saying to myself. I was out of breath as I stepped up and onto the dunes that spread over this area of the inlet. He was there, sitting by the graves of Sam and the pelican. I looked around; no one had seen me. No one else was out. I walked over and sat down beside him.

"Sam was a good dog," I said.

"Yeah, he was," he responded.

"I'm sorry about your family." He stared straight ahead. "Mrs. Jackson told me. That had to have been awful for you."

"You don't know who I am. What I am," he said, still not looking at me.

"You are right. There is a lot I don't know, but you are going to answer those questions. What I do know is you pulled me up out of the water. I would have drowned. I saw you with Mrs. Jackson. We buried Sam right here. You care about people. I don't think I could be that kind if I'd lost my family."

"You don't know me!" Suddenly he was angry.

"Then tell me!" I said. "Who is Ben Smith? And what is his connection with the lights in the water, and does any of what is happening have to do with that? I know you know. I've seen the lights. What was it in the water? Something was in the water with me. I could feel it. I could see the light. What was it? My leg hurt, Ben. You fixed it. I don't know how, but you did. Talk to me!" I was almost pleading with him for answers.

He stood and walked a few feet away. "If I ask you to trust me and believe what I tell you, will you?" he said to me still not looking at me.

"Why don't you tell me, and I'll decide if I believe you or not," I answered him as I stood and walked to where he was.

"Do you see that star … right there?" He pointed to the night sky.

"I did not come out to look at the stars, Ben." I was beginning to sound annoyed.

"Right there … second from the moon," he insisted.

I looked and focused on the bright star he was referring to. "Yes, I see it. Stop dodging my questions."

"Ben Smith is from Michigan. I am from there," he said, still pointing to the second star from the moon.

"Right. And I'm from Venus. Nice try, but insanity will not work."

"Your planet has water. Lots of it. Ours is drying up. I came in search of water, and I found it."

"Wait, wait, wait!" I shook my head and began to laugh. "You seriously think I came out here to listen to this … bull? The authorities can ask you about the lights." I turned to walk away, frustrated at his nonsense.

"I'll show you," he said.

Oh, this had better be good, I thought and stopped and turned back to look at him. "How? How can you prove such stupidity?"

He walked over to me. "Trust me—that I won't hurt you and that I will answer your questions," he said as he stood in front of me.

"Great. And it better be good." I looked at him, waiting.

He took my hand; I pulled back reluctantly. "Trust me," he said again. I let him take my hand and place it on his heart.

"Yes, you are alive," I said sarcastically as I felt his heart beat under my hand. I tried to pull away, but he held it there.

"I feel emotion because Ben felt emotion. I'm compassionate because Ben was compassionate. I am here, because of Ben," he said, not letting go of my hand.

"That doesn't make sense," I said to him. "You are Ben."

"No, Ben saved my life. I was in the water. I could not survive out of the water. Ben was dying, drowning with the rest of them. I entered his body, so he saved my life. I could do nothing to save his."

I just stood there in disbelief of what he was saying. *Okay, maybe this is how he deals with reality*, I thought to myself.

"Do I feel normal to you?" he asked and pressed my hand harder to his chest. "Does this feel normal to you?" he asked as he leaned forward and kissed me. I was so stunned I could not move. The kiss was over, and he released my hand from his heart and stepped a few feet away from me. I could not say anything. I was still tingling from the kiss. I looked at him standing there in the moonlight, and it was as if my eyes began to blur.

"Trust me," he said again as his body began to … began to become … I don't know … a light of some kind, from his head to his toes. A vapor of some sort of energy.

He walked over to me. I instinctively backed away, but could hear him say "Trust me," so I stopped. He again took my hand and placed it on his chest. I could still feel his heartbeat, and then the light energy began to fade, and he was standing there in front of me.

"I don't understand."

"I'm both," he said. "I'm not human, and I'm not what I was. I can't go back, and we cannot survive on this planet in our form, out of the water."

"But you are! I'm so confused! Is this real?"

"In this environment, our kind cannot survive unless we take on human form, then we can adapt. That was not our intent when I came here, but it all went wrong. I couldn't get back, and I was dying, and there was Ben. I did not even know if he could handle my energy without killing us both. But it did. And now they have come."

"They?" I asked, still in disbelief, but I knew he was telling me the truth.

"What I've done is a terrible thing. This planet could not sustain us, but now I've shown that it can work if we take on human form. They have not come to take me home. They have come to stay. I've tried to convince them, but our planet is desperate. They are dying there. Many die on the journey, and we can only survive in the water, getting our energy from its life forms. But the results of that will destroy this planet."

"Stop," I said. It was all too much for me. I wished I had stayed home. I wished I had gone to Wyoming. Anywhere but here and what was happening right now. I couldn't believe what I had just heard, but I had to believe it. It was real. The unbelievable was real. "The lights?" I asked him as I stood and looked out at the water.

"Hundreds of them," he said.

I expected to look out and see them, like stars in the sky, but there was nothing but blackness and the sound of the crashing waves.

"You can't go to the authorities," he said as we stood there still looking at the blackness of the water. "Not yet."

"So what? You can read my mind too?" I asked him as I thought that was exactly what I'd have to do.

"I need time to convince them that we need to look somewhere else. That staying here we could eventually die anyway," he said.

"Could? But not if you are human? Not that you *are* human … oh my God … I can't believe I'm even having this conversation. This cannot be happening." I sank to my knees and sat with my hands covering my face.

"I wish it were not happening," he said and sat beside me. "I wish I had not made it through the entry. I wish I had been strong enough to resist the life-giving energy Ben had to offer. I wish I had not been able to survive here even in this body. But I need time before it is too late," he said, still looking at the water. His words shocked me back to reality.

"I have to try to understand this," I said to him. "If it is possible for me to understand, you have to start at the beginning. How did you get here?" I asked him as I looked at the stars in the cloudless night sky.

"I can't expect you to understand, but I ask you to trust me. I'm telling you the truth." I didn't want to, but somehow, I knew that he was telling me the truth. Chills ran up my spine as he recounted his journey from his home that was not like here. A vapor-like atmosphere where their life came from energy from the sun and their need for water. A life form—not like here on earth but an intelligent life form dependent on the sun, but the sun itself was drying up the water vapor that was their very form. "A team was sent out. There were others with me," he recounted. "Hoping that together, our energy would be enough to enter through your atmosphere and we would survive or there would be enough of us to find water and still be able to go back so others could come." I listened in amazement as he continued, "The friction of the atmosphere destroyed all of us, except for me. Our mission was a failure, and I hoped they would not try another when I found myself immersed in the waters of the Atlantic Ocean, just off this coast. The water was a comfort and soothing in my death. And then there was Ben, fighting to stay above water. I found him as his body could not fight anymore and he slipped beneath the water. I had just a moment to decide …" There was a long pause. "I should have let him die there with his family, and I should have died just like the rest of mine. And now I have brought them here."

I felt like I should comfort him in some way, but I just couldn't move. "We draw our energy from the water and the life forms in it, killing them while we live. The only way to exist outside the water is to find something that is strong enough to accept our energy. I did that. I did that … I don't know if I can stop them."

"We have to go to the authorities." I snapped to reality and stood looking down on him.

"Huh." He halfway laughed. "What good would that do? Even if they believed me, they would do what? Lock me up?" He stood as he continued. "It's up to me, *me* … to convince them—us—that death is better than life." He turned away and looked out at the water.

"They could keep everyone out of the water. Ben, we can't let people go back into the water. How do you know that it is just you who … who …"

"It's just me," he answered before I could finish.

"How long have they been here?"

"Not long, and so far, the fish and birds have been enough."

"So far," I repeated his words. "But for how long, Ben?"

"As long as it takes." He seemed angry again. "It's my fault, and I will fix it." There was so much sorrow in his voice. I felt compelled to touch him. I touched his back as I stood behind him. I leaned forward until my head rested on the back of his neck. "You saved me. You'll figure a way," I said to him, and I somehow believed it.

"Even if we are able to keep everyone out of the water, we'll destroy the ocean, and as our energy gets stronger, the ocean will heat up and—"

"You will convince them … you will. After all, you convinced me that you are not a moron, and a few days ago, that was an impossibility." I could feel his body untense. He turned to face me.

"And you are definitely not a princess." He smiled as he touched my hair. Suddenly he pushed me to the sand and fell on the ground beside me. "Shhh," he said before I could respond. A spotlight was scanning around, and the sound of the engine shut off.

"I know I saw them," one of them said. I could not see who it was but was sure it was beach patrol or authorities of some sort. I tried to raise my head, but Ben pushed my face almost into the sand. I looked at him; he just put his finger to his lips to keep silent. "They went into the water … somewhere right here."

"I don't see a thing," the other voice said. "Hey!" he yelled. "Anyone out there? This is the police. Out of the water!" There was a silence.

"I don't know. I know I saw something," the first man said.

"Maybe the dark is playing tricks on you," the other said. "No. I know what I saw. Shine the light again. Okay, let's head back."

The engine of the four-wheeler started, and when it was far enough away, Ben unleashed his grip on me. I turned over and lay face up in the sand. He lay there beside me, looking up at the stars.

"Do you have family?" I asked him.

"They drowned in the boating accident," he responded.

"Not Ben. You."

He paused before he said, "Not like you. Not like here. We are all the same. We are all alike. We are all family, I guess." He was sad again.

"I don't think you are all alike at all," I said. "If you were, you would have let them take me. That is what was happening in the water, wasn't it? The light I saw. You could have let it happen, but you didn't because you are not like that."

"What am I like … it's okay for me but not for them? How can I justify that? How can I convince them?"

"There have to be others who will feel the same way as you! You can convince them to find another place. That this is not the answer. You can! I know you can! Trust me!" I said to him.

"When you say that, I almost believe that I can." He sat up and looked at me. He leaned down until his lips were a few inches from mine, pausing as if waiting for me to resist. I did not. I did not want to; I wanted him to kiss me—this time because he wanted to, not to prove something to me. His lips touched mine. Softly at first, his lips brushed across mine. Then he kissed me … gently. It was over before I wanted it to be.

"You should have gone to Wyoming," he said as he got up and walked toward the beach.

"Hey!" I said as I got up to follow him. "How do you know about Wyoming?" I asked, forgetting for a moment that yes, he probably could read my mind. Why not? As we stepped down onto the beach, we saw them at the same time. Two people were coming up out of the water. "What are they doing in the water?" I asked as Ben and I stopped and the figures were coming closer.

The closer they came, I recognized one of them to be the man from the other day. The one who had almost drowned and … "Mr. Carlton?" I asked out loud. It was Mr. Carlton. They were walking right toward us. Ben had not said a word. They walked right past us, up onto the marsh, and did not say a word.

"Ben, they were just in the water." He was just looking at the water where they had come from. "Ben!" I said to him again.

"Go through over the dunes to the road and go home, Christi. Stay in until you are cleared." He had my shoulders in his hands, looking me in the eyes. "Promise me you will stay away from the water," he said.

"What are you going to do, Ben? I'm scared."

He turned and walked away from me into the water. "Ben!" I called him as I followed him to the water's edge. "Ben!" I said again as he dove into the water. There was a part of me that wanted to go into the water after him, a subconscious longing almost. I turned and walked to the dunes. I stood for a moment and looked at the water. Where was he? And then I saw it—the light.

PART TWO

Chapter Seven

The stars in the night sky were as brilliant as I had ever seen them. The moon was not quite full, but the luminous glow lit up the night, and I could see down the beach toward the beachfront houses. Houses full of families who lived there and those who chose this beach to vacation on this week. People who were being asked to stay off the beach and could not leave until authorities figured out what was going on here. I thought about all those people as I sat there in the moonlight. *If they only knew*, I thought to myself and realized that before long, they would know. Everyone would know. As crazy as it had all sounded as Ben had tried to explain how he got here and what was happening, I knew he was telling me the truth. And I knew that as awful as the events of the last few days had been, it was going to get worse.

I had to go to the authorities and tell them what I knew, but they would probably lock me up. *I* would lock me up. Just as Ben had said, I had to give him a little time to … to do what? I looked out over the water. No lights. No sign of Ben since he had gone out into the waves—oh, it must have been an hour ago. "Go home," he had said to me before he disappeared in the water. "I'm not leaving!" I had yelled to him before the light faded. "If I have to sit here all night," I had whispered to myself when the light was gone and I sat down in the sand and stared at the crashing waves. I had not moved for an hour, scanning the water for any sign of Ben … lights … anything. I had to wait for him. He couldn't tell me something like that and then just expect me to go home and get a good night's sleep.

I thought of Aunt Abby—sleeping peacefully I hoped. I felt bad about sneaking out and wished I had just stayed home. I wouldn't have heard any of this. I wouldn't have seen Mr. Carlton and the other guy come out of the water. "Unbelievable," I said out loud as I thought about Mr. Carlton. Two days ago he had been confined to a wheelchair; tonight, he had walked right by me as if he didn't even see me. What did Ben mean when he said it was happening? I asked myself as I scanned the beach in case Ben was to come ashore somewhere further down the beach.

Too late for what—or did I want to know? "Ugh," I said out loud as I lay back on the sand. "I'm making myself crazy." I looked up into the night sky. It was like looking at a velvet blanket with pinholes all through it where light was coming through. "I am from there." His words ran over and over in my mind as I looked at the second star from the moon. Could this really be happening? Suddenly my eyes filled with tears. Nothing would ever be the same, even if we would be allowed to leave. I know. Things would continue to get worse just as Ben said. And soon the water would not contain them.

I sat straight up, and my body began to shiver. Mr. Carlton, he was one of them somehow ... like Ben. Oh my God! And the other man, the one from the first day of tryouts. He had been drowning in the water ... with the lights. The thoughts made me nauseous and made my hair stand on end. It was the only explanation for Mr. Carlton being able to walk. Only it wasn't Mr. Carlton at all. Even Mrs. Carlton could sense something strange about him, not to mention the miracle of his walking.

How many others? I wondered. The water had been full of people all week. I couldn't think about it. Ben would know what to do. He had to, I told myself as the sound of the tide broke the silence of the early morning stillness. I looked again into the night sky to the star where the impossible was reality. Wait. Where was it? I blinked to clear my eyes and focused again. First on the moon. First star. "Where is it?" I said out loud and stood to my feet. It was not there. I scanned the sky. Stars, all as bright as they had been all night. Only this time, it was gone.

"Christi, you really are going crazy!" I said to myself. But it was not there. It had been distinctive, bright, almost stood out. Now there was emptiness where it had been. I felt sick again, like I was going to throw up. "Calm down. Concentrate," I told myself as I looked again for the star that Ben had called home. It was gone. It seemed as impossible as everything else that had happened, but it was not there. I sat back down and put my face in my hands. "Please, God. Let this all be a dream."

I lay there listening to the sound of the waves, then the dreams came. I was in the water, sinking, fighting at first, struggling to surface for air, just to sink again, lights all around me, drawing me in. As if they would save me. If I would just let them. I would struggle against the temptation to give in, surface, only to sink all over again. Again, like in the dreams before, I did not fight it. I did not want to. "Let go," I told myself. "It's okay, Christi," someone was telling me. As I sank deeper under the water, the lights surrounded me. Coming closer, I could feel the warmth from them. I was drowning, and they were life. *Let them in*, I told myself. *Let them in*. And then I was being pulled up out of the water by someone. Just like before. I broke the surface of the water, gasping for air, and was pulled to shore, only this time the person that saved me was right there beside me.

It was Ben. He looked at me. "Christi, are you okay?" I couldn't speak. I just looked at him. "Christi?" I was awakened by someone touching my arm. I raised my head to see Ben sitting beside me. "I thought I told you to go home hours ago," he said as he looked at me.

I couldn't say anything. I just threw my arms around him and started to cry. He gently pulled me to him as I laid my head on his chest. "Tell me it's going to be okay,"

I said to him, almost pleading with him. "Ben," I said as I pulled away enough that I could look into his eyes. His eyes were filling with tears as he stared out at the water. "It's going to be okay, right?" I asked again and waited for him to respond.

"They have to know what is coming," he said as he stood.

"What's coming?" I repeated what he had said. "Ben, what's coming?"

He turned and headed down the beach without another word of explanation. *Oh no, you don't*, I thought to myself and headed after him, half running to catch up with him. "Tell me, Ben," I said to him as I caught up with him and pulled on his arm. "I have a right to know," I pleaded with him, but he just pulled away and quickened his stride, leaving me standing there in the darkness. "I know about Mr. Carlton, Ben!" I yelled to him. "And the other guy. I can't just pretend I didn't see them!" I was still yelling, but it was as if he did not even hear me.

He was far enough down the beach I could no longer see him as I still just stood there in the blackness of the night with only the sound of the crashing waves as the tide had begun to go back out. *That's it*, I thought to myself. *I will sit here. He won't leave me here. He'll come back, and he'll have to talk to me.* I sat down on the wet sand right where I had stood and looked out into the black water, knowing any second Ben would be right beside me.

Annoyed, yes, but he would come back, and I would convince him to tell everything. I knew too much for him not to tell me what was coming or what was going to happen, whatever it was he had said. What did he mean by that? He would explain it … when he came back for me. As the minutes passed, I noticed that the wind had started to pick up. I hugged my knees to my chest as the cool breeze off the water chilled me as I sat in the darkness. I looked into the night sky, and I not only couldn't see *the* star, I couldn't see any stars! The sky was as black as the ocean. Just then, I saw a flash of lightning off in the distance.

"Great," I said out loud and stood to my feet. Another storm was coming. *Moron*, I thought to myself as I started down the beach toward Aunt Abby's house. Another flash of lightning and clap of thunder shook the ground as the clouds let loose and rain started to pour. I made a run for it; the beach house was at least a mile away. An occasional lightning flash was the only light available to see where I was.

It has to be still the early hours of the morning, I thought. How long was I in the marsh waiting for Ben? How long had I been asleep? Long enough to have the dream. I looked out over the water. A flash of lightning lit up the beach, but it was too late. I ran into—stumbled over—something and went sprawling head first out onto to the sand. "Ohhhh!" I moaned out loud and grabbed my ankle. "What the heck?" I looked to see what had whacked me in the shin. I strained to see what looked to be a log left behind by the tide, but as a flash of lightning again lit up the sky, I saw what it was. I screamed as I realized what I had fallen over was a dolphin. A dolphin whose body had been left behind by the tide.

I tried to stand, but my ankle gave way. I scooted myself away from the dolphin until I was a few feet away. I rubbed my ankle with one hand and tried to wipe rain and the tears from my face with the other. As the storm was getting more and more intense, I again tried to stand. Pain shot up my leg, but I managed to put enough weight on it that I could walk or hobble toward Aunt Abby's. The sky continued to be lit up by lightning, and all along the water's edge, dead fish were being left by the receding waves. "My God," I said as I stepped over fish after fish after fish, so many more than this morning.

As I pulled myself up the steps of the beach house, I saw the lights at the Carltons' were on. The garage apartment was dark. Was Ben even there? Maybe he had already gone to the authorities? I sat down on the porch and gently began to rub my ankle again. It was just a sprain, but that meant no running or swimming for a while. "Are you crazy?" I thought out loud, remembering that the days ahead would be anything but normal. No running on the beach. No one allowed at the beach. And definitely no one in the water. Just then the porch light came on. I was blinded and startled by the sudden light.

"Christi?" I heard Aunt Abby say. "What are you doing out here? It's three o'clock in the morning!" She came out the screen door. I was startled and jumped to my feet as Aunt Abby came onto the porch, and my ankle gave way as I let out a yell and grabbed it in pain. "Oh, Luvy … I'm so sorry! I didn't mean to scare you! Are you okay?" she said as she sat down beside me. "Is it your ankle? Did you twist it?" she asked.

"I … think … so," I said.

"Here, let's get inside. Let me help you." I stood and was able to put weight on my ankle as Aunt Abby took my arm to help steady me. I looked back at the beach, knowing what we would find in the morning light as again lightning flashed and the thunder rumbled the porch.

"Wait," I said to her as I stood looking out at the water. "Do you see that, Aunt Abby? There in the water … were lights."

"See what, Luvy?" she asked as she turned to look at what I was talking about.

"There in the water. Lights. Dozens of them." I looked at her as she stared out at the water. "I've seen them before, Aunt Abby. They are in the water. It's Ben, Mr. Carlton, the dead fish, the dolphin. It all has to do with the lights somehow."

"Luvy, it's so late. You are so tired. Let's get to bed," she said as she started toward the door.

"No! The lights, Aunt Abby. Don't you see the lights?" She stopped as she looked at me, turned to look toward the ocean and the lights that were a few hundred yards off-shore. She looked out at them as I stood beside her, seeing the dozens of lights, like stars in the water shining in the midst of the storm.

"I don't see anything, Luvy," she said. "Let's get inside." She pulled me as I limped across the porch and into the house. I insisted I could make it to my room, so we limped up the stairs and into my room without saying anything.

"Can you get changed and into bed okay?"

"Yes. Thanks, Aunt Abby."

"Good night, Luvy. Love you," she said.

"To the moon and back," I said as she closed the door. I got out of my rain-soaked clothes and grabbed a T-shirt from my drawer. I then hobbled over to the window, raised it up, and pulled in the rope ladder and returned it to the closet. Aunt Abby may have questions tomorrow, but for tonight, or at least what was left of it, she didn't know anything. As I closed the window and as the beads of rain started to run down the pane, I said out loud, "Why can't Abby see you?" as I looked at the black water dotted with lights.

Chapter Eight

I put my finger on the glass and traced a drop of rain as it ran down the windowpane, making a path to the bottom of the frame collecting other drops on its way. An occasional flash of lightning lit up the sky. I just stood there watching the lights, expecting each time that I blinked to open my eyes and find that they were gone. But they remained, and it seemed as though there were more and more, only closer together now, so that it was more of a glow under the surface of the water than the individual lights.

If Aunt Abby can't see them, then why can I? I asked myself, knowing I did not have the answer. *Maybe she was just too tired. After all, it was three o'clock in the morning.* I glanced at the clock on my bedside table—4:18 a.m., it read—and I quickly focused my eyes on the white glow that was illuminating an even bigger area now.

"Surely I'm not the only one who sees this?" I asked out loud, trying to convince myself I was not, yet also rationalizing the possibility of what it could mean if I was the only one seeing them. *Three days ago, my life seemed so … normal. Now it is anything but normal,* I thought as I recounted in my mind the events of the last three days.

My encounter with Ben at the airport (*Moron,* I thought to myself and managed a smile), being here with Aunt Abby, the dead fish, the dead birds, Sam, Mr. Carlton, Ben, the lights, "What's coming," the last words Ben had said.

He wasn't talking about the lights. They are already here. What could be coming? I asked myself the question again, knowing I did not have the answer. Ben knew the answer, but he wasn't talking … to me anyway. If he wasn't talking to the authorities now, he would be soon. Would they believe him? What would they do if they did? He would have to convince them some way, I thought. They would think he was some crazy, attention-seeking moron coming to them with some crazy story of star travel and an intelligence … energy … substance … being. "Of course they will think he is crazy," I said out loud. *Show them the lights,* I thought and then realized that if Aunt Abby couldn't see them, maybe no one could, except me.

My eyes were fixated on the glow in the water a few hundred yards offshore that was definitely growing larger. *He will have to show them, like he did to me,* I thought as I recounted in my mind the disbelief I felt as I had watched

Ben's body become a vapor with a spiritlike glow and the feeling I had as my hand felt his heartbeat and the tingling I felt as his lips had kissed me.

I wiped a tear that had spilled out onto my cheek and again followed a raindrop as it snaked a path down the windowpane. The rain had not let up, and the wind had gained strength as the palm trees and sea grass swayed in its path. What if he couldn't make them believe? Or worse, what if they did believe him? Would they lock him up? Just like he had said. Use him as some … some experiment. Use his energy some way.

Suddenly I thought of Mr. Carlton, what had happened to him because of the lights. Whatever they were, he had something happen to him somehow, and look at him now. I had seen him three days ago unable to walk, and tonight I stood as he walked right past me as he came out of the water, along with the other man, the man from the tryouts—he had been drowning, and now he was in the water with Mr. Carlton. If contact with the lights had made Mr. Carlton able to walk, then what could they do if they decided to contain them and use them? Could they be sold to the highest bidder, to someone who was terminal, as a way of renewing life, prolonging life? I shuddered as so many thoughts raced through my head.

I had to trust that Ben knew what he was doing. I hoped he had decided to wait until morning to go to the authorities. The sun would be coming up in a couple of hours. I would be at the Carltons' first thing. I would try to convince Ben that there must be another way. I could only wait and hope and pray. "Dear God," I said as I closed my eyes for the first time since I had gotten into my room and stood in my window, watching for … I was not sure how long. "I know that you are real, and I know that nothing happens that you are not aware of, that nothing happens unless you allow it to, so you must have a reason or a purpose for what is happening right here. I'm asking, Lord, if it be your will, then please protect Ben."

As I opened my eyes, the rain on the window had made the lights in the water seem like a hazy blur. "Amen," I finished out loud, and at the same instant, the lights were gone. Just like that … like someone had turned off a switch. I rubbed the windowpane, as if the raindrops were on the inside and rubbing it would make it clearer, but they were not there. Only the occasional light from a flash of lightning but only blackness in the water.

The sun would be up soon. The thought of what would remain on the beach when the water receded with what the light of the day would reveal sickened me, and I turned away from the window. It was 5:30 a.m. I hobbled around the side of my bed and sat on the edge as I reached for my cell phone. It was still in the rain-soaked shorts I had had on. "Great," I said as I wiped it off and hoped it would work. "Mom," I said as I heard her voice say hello on the other end.

"Christi, honey, are you okay?"

"I'm okay, Mom." I stopped her. "I just wanted to hear your voice."

"Honey, Abby assured me everything was okay. That you would be leaving today probably. Do you want me to come get you? I can leave first thing—"

"Mom, Mom, it's okay. I'm sorry, I forgot it's still the middle of the night out there. Everything is fine. I'm sure we will be leaving soon. I'll let you know when we do. Love you."

"Love you too, honey," I heard her say as I ended the call.

I would call my dad later. No need to wake him up too. I had not slept all night, but somehow, I did not feel tired at all. Besides, I couldn't sleep now. I would be at the Carltons' as soon as it was light. I had to talk to Ben before … I let my thoughts trail off as I went into the bathroom and started the shower.

I smell like fish, I thought to myself as I stepped into the warm water from the rain showerhead. What would I say to Ben? How could I talk to him about something I didn't even understand myself? I had to trust him … but what if? Thoughts kept running over and over in my head. I couldn't make them stop.

"Stay out of it, Christi. I know what I am doing." I was startled by the voice in my head. I turned off the water and stood quietly.

"Ben?" I asked out loud, knowing the voice I had heard, Ben's voice, had been in my head but also had seemed so real. "Get a grip," I said to myself as I stepped out of the shower and wrapped a towel around my hair. As I pulled some clothes from my dresser drawer, I could see that the sun was beginning to come up—no bright sunshine, just light through the clouds of the storm that was still hanging on.

I ran down the stairs and grabbed a rain jacket from the closet and started for the porch. "No," I said out loud and turned to go out the front door instead. I did not want to see what I knew I would be on the beach this morning. I decided I would leave a note for Aunt Abby. After last night, I had escaped questioning, so on a notepad I scribbled "At the Carltons' ... be right back" and slid out the front door, gently closing it behind me.

As soon as it closed, I ran down the stairs, down the drive, the few yards to the Carltons' driveway, and up the steps to the garage apartment. As I rang the doorbell and knocked at the same time, it suddenly dawned on me that my ankle was fine. I had totally forgotten it. I looked down at it as if to make sure it was there.

As I knocked on the door, I could feel my heart start to pound in my chest. No answer could mean that Ben was not there or that he just did not want to talk to me.

"Ben!" I yelled as I knocked again and turned the knob on the door, expecting to find it locked, but instead it turned, and I opened the door. "Ben!" I said again as I stepped inside, leaving the door open behind me. He was not here; it looked as if no one had ever been here. It was perfect, everything neatly in its place. Nothing was out of place. I stepped into the bathroom. Towels hung neatly on the racks. I walked back into the bedroom where the bed was neatly made. Sides were tucked in. Pillows were arranged perfectly.

What guy lives like this? I asked myself. *None I've ever seen. All my friends' brothers are slobs when it comes to their rooms.* But something caught my eye. It was on the night-stand beside the bed, a photo in a frame. I walked over and picked up the picture. It was a picture of Ben and his family—his mom, dad, and sister. They were all standing in front of a boat. It looked like it must have been taken sometime just before the accident, because Ben looked just as he did now.

Just then, a gust of wind whirled through the open door and then sucked the door shut, slamming it so hard I screamed and dropped the picture frame onto the tiled floor, which shattered into little pieces, leaving the photo lying among the broken pieces. "Oh no!" I said out loud and bent down and started to pick up the mess I had made. The one thing Ben had to remember his family. I thought, *At least the picture is fine. I can replace the frame.*

I placed the picture on the nightstand where it had been, picked up the pieces of glass with the broken frame, and placed it in the trash can from the bathroom. I would tell him what had happened and replace the frame.

As I walked out of the apartment, I knew that at least Ben had planned or expected he would be back. If not, he would never have left the picture behind. I was sure of that. Maybe he had said something to the Carltons—or had Mr. Carlton even come home after I had seen him the night before? I walked down the steps of the garage apartment and across the deck to the front door of the Carltons' and rang the doorbell. After a few seconds, Nancy Carlton opened the door.

"Christi, what a surprise!" She opened the door wider so I could come inside. "Bob, look who's come to visit," she said as I stepped into their entryway. "Let me take your jacket."

"It's okay, Mrs. Carlton, I can't stay long," I said as I saw Mr. Carlton standing in the living room looking out the window, just like he had the last time I was here. "Hi, Mr. Carlton, how are you today?" I asked, but he did not seem to know that I was even there. He just kept staring out at the water.

"He's just been watching all the activity out there this morning." Nancy said as she walked over and stood beside him. "Lots of dead fish. The news is reporting something about a fault line … maybe somehow up the water. I don't know—I can't understand all of it. Bob is the scientific one, aren't you, honey?" she said to him, but his expression never changed.

I walked over and looked out the big sliding doors that faced the ocean and saw that there were people in hazmat suits all over the beach scooping up dead fish and birds from the sand, and again, samples of the water were being collected. Men were posting warning signs all along the beach: BEACH CLOSED. DO NOT ENTER THE WATER.

"Have you heard anything from the authorities, Mrs. Carlton? About when we can leave?" I asked.

"No, not yet," she answered. "But I don't think we will be going anywhere. It's the one thing Bob has made clear: he will not leave our home here."

"What about your home in Michigan?" I asked, thinking that they are only here for a few weeks out of the summer anyway.

"I don't know," she said with a sadness in her voice. "I'm afraid if we leave, I will lose him again." She gently put her arm around Mr. Carlton and laid her head on his shoulder. He still made no move but just continued to look out the window.

"I was looking for Ben. He is not in the apartment. Have you seen him this morning?" I asked her, feeling pretty sure they had not.

"No, but he often goes out early. Did you need something?"

"No, it's okay. I just wanted to see if he had heard anything … about when we are allowed to leave and all," I said as I turned to leave. "Mrs. Carlton, can I ask you a question?"

"Sure, Christi, but call me Nancy." She smiled and sat down on the couch and patted the seat beside her for me to sit down. I took the spot beside her as I decided I would use the opportunity to learn more about Ben.

"How long have you guys known Ben?"

"Oh, we've known his family since we've been coming here for vacations, even before we bought this house from the Wilsons. Terrible thing, the accident. He was already planning to apply at Michigan, so after graduation and after what happened, him having no other family and all, it just seemed the thing to do. He's been with us on breaks and has been like a grandson to us ever since. And such a big help with Bob." She glanced over at Mr. Carlton, who had not moved. "Since his stroke, I could not have managed without Ben. And now …" Tears began to well up in her eyes as she talked about what they had been through. "I just can't believe that he is standing there." Her tears spilled over and down her cheeks.

"It shows that you should never give up," I said as I stood and leaned over to give her a hug. "Thanks, Mrs. Carlton, uh … Nancy." I smiled as I walked toward the door. "Oh, one more thing." I turned to ask her, "Have you noticed anything in the water … at night?"

"In the water?" she asked. "No … like what?" She sounded curious.

"Like … lights … in the water," I said. There was silence as Mrs. Carlton and I looked at Mr. Carlton at the same time. He had slowly turned to face us, looked me in the eyes, and said, "Yes, I have seen the lights."

I froze as a chill ran the whole length of my spine. I could not even speak. I just stood there staring at Mr. Carlton, who had said what he wanted to say and had turned back to face the view that seemed to have him in a trance or something.

"Bob?" Mrs. Carlton said as she went to his side. "This is great. This is progress. Oh, honey," she continued. "I'm so proud of you." She put her arms around the man she loved so much. The man she thought he was … or who he used to be.

"Can you tell me what you saw, Mr. Carlton?" I asked him, but he was nonresponsive again. "The lights? Can you tell me when you saw the lights?" Nothing. He just stared out at the water. "Mrs. Carlton, the day that Mr. Carlton stood—" I started to ask.

"It was a miracle!" she said and patted his back.

"Did anything happen before that? Out of the ordinary, I mean … anything before he got up that morning and walked downstairs?" I asked.

"No …" She thought out loud, "Oh, maybe it was nothing." She stopped.

"What? Please go on," I said to her.

"Well, I didn't notice it at first. It was after our water therapy session. I had helped Bob that day. Ben was training me on what to do and how to hold him while I exercised his arms and legs. It was after we came in and we were getting ready for bed … I noticed this," she said as she pointed down to Mr. Carlton's leg. "On the side of his leg. It looked like a cut of some kind. I tried to put something on it, but Bob wouldn't let me. It was the first time since the stroke that he was able to communicate with me. See, it's all better now." She rubbed the scar where the cut had been. "Everything is better now," she repeated and stood there beside him.

"Tell Ben I need to see him if he comes in, will you, Mrs. Carlton?"

"Of course. Tell Abby to come by before you leave," she said as I walked out their front door. My hand was shaking so hard I could hardly close the door. I was shaking all over as I stood facing the closed door, not sure I could even move.

"Christi!" I heard Aunt Abby yell from the front porch.

"Coming!"

Chapter Nine

"Is Bob okay, Luvy?" Aunt Abby asked as I climbed the steps to the porch of the beach house, where she was waiting for me.

"Yes, I guess ... he still just stands there looking at the water," I answered her, not wanting to mention the lights for fear it may bring up more questions about the night before. "Mrs. Carlton said she heard something on the news about maybe the fault line having something to do with what is killing the fish?" I half stated, half asked as we both went into the house closing the door behind us.

"Yes," she said. "That was the report. They are saying the water is testing okay, but it just keeps getting hotter and hotter. It seems as if it is the only explanation for now. But not contamination, thank God, so we don't have to worry about that. They are still testing though. I saw them out there this morning, and sooo many fish! It's just awful." She shook her head and walked over to the windows looking out to the beach. "They said all restrictions will be lifted today, Luvy, so I'm going to call and see if we can get a flight out this eve—"

"No! We can't leave!" I blurted out before she could finish. "Not yet," I finished as Aunt Abby turned to look at me.

"Luvy, we can't get into the water, and we don't want to wake up every morning to dead birds and fish and the smell! It's horrible what is happening, but there's nothing we can do. I've told John we would leave as soon as we could. He's worried, Luvy, and so is your dad. You need to call him."

"I had planned to, and I will, but, Aunt Abby, please—we only have a few more days left anyway. It's not going to hurt us to stay. We've not even had any time for the two of us. Please, Aunt Abby?" I pleaded with her.

"We'll make up for it this summer. I promise."

"Just a couple of days," I begged.

"We should hear from the mayor's office soon. You should finish packing," she said as she turned from the window and looked at me. My eyes were spilling over with tears. "Luvy," she said and started to walk toward me. I turned and ran across the room and started up the stairs without saying another word. "Looks like your ankle is better," I heard her say as I slammed my door.

I flung myself on my bed. *This can't be happening*, I said to myself. *Not now. We can't leave now. Ben, I have to know what is going on with him ... with ...* I put my pillow over my face as the tears began to soak it. The thought of leaving, knowing what I knew and not really knowing what was happening or what was going to happen, was enough. But to think I wouldn't see Ben before we left or might not ever see him again was too much.

The tears came like the rain. I turned over on my side and stared at the picture on my nightstand. It was of Aunt Abby and me; I was only five. We were playing on the beach that day it was taken by Uncle John. She was standing, looking down at me as I had finished drawing a heart in the sand with our names in it. I dried my tears, sat up with my back against the head board, and took a breath before reaching for my cell phone.

"Hey, Dad," I said as I heard his voice on the other end.

"Hey, honey. I'm so glad to hear your voice. It seems like I haven't heard it for weeks now …"

"Oh, Dad, it's only been a few days," I said, knowing we would always go through this when I was away from him.

"Well, you can't get home soon enough for me. Not been a very good trip for you two. I've been seeing all the dead fish on the news. You are not going in the water, are you?" he asked.

"No, Dad, not since they started washing up. They're saying the water temperature is rising. Is that what you are hearing?" I asked him.

"Yeah. Can't pinpoint the cause yet, but they will. Hear you are getting some bad weather too," he said.

"Yes," I said as I looked at the window and the rain was still pouring and running down the pane.

"Abby says you are getting a flight out soon, so text me the info. I'll be there. I'm ready for you to come home." I couldn't say anything. "Honey, are you there?" he asked.

"I'll let you know. Bye, Dad." I managed to get out and hang up the phone and throw it on the nightstand. It slid across and knocked the picture of Aunt Abby and me off the nightstand. "Not again!" I said out loud as I got up to retrieve the picture. *At least it did not break*, I thought as I placed it back on the stand. "Oh! It's perfect!" I said and began to take the back off the frame, remove the picture, put the picture in the drawer of the nightstand, and run out of the room and down the stairs where Aunt Abby was on the phone. "Be right back!" I said to her as she glanced at me, still talking on the phone—to the airlines rep I'm sure.

I ran out the door and down the steps in the pouring rain with no jacket. I had taken it off on my dash up the stairs to my room. *Great*, I thought as I tucked the wood frame under my blouse as I ran down the drive to the Carltons' to the stairs to the garage apartment. I turned the knob of the door and found it the same as before—unlocked—so I stepped inside.

I grabbed a sweatshirt from the hook beside the door and put it on. "A Michigan sweatshirt! Eeeewww!" I said and thought about not putting it on, but it was warm and I was dripping all over the floor. I went into the bedroom and put the picture of Ben and his family into the frame I had brought with me.

I have to explain, I thought, so I opened the drawer of the nightstand to see if there might be a pad of paper and a pen. There wasn't, but there was a book. As I took it out, I realized it was a photo album. I sat down on the side of the bed and opened it. It was a collection of pictures of Ben's family—when he was little, at Christmas, birthdays, at the beach, here.

As I closed the album and started to place it back in the drawer, I noticed a box in the bottom underneath where the album had been. I wondered if I should take it out, if I had the right to snoop in Ben's private things. I sat the box on my lap and untied the string that had secured the lid and lifted the lid off the box. It was filled with papers and letters. I unfolded one of the sheets of paper to see it was a letter he had written to his mom from camp.

"I'm fine, don't worry," he had told her. "Be home soon. Love, your son."

I smiled and wiped away tears as I folded the letter and placed it back in the box. There was his acceptance letter to Michigan and a card that was clipped to it: "From Mom and Dad. We are so proud of you!" they had written. I flipped, threw the contents of the box, and pulled out a card. It had a little girl and boy on the front. They were playing on the beach, building a sand castle. The inside read, "Happy birthday to the best brother ever." My eyes again spilled over with tears as I put the lid back on the box, tied the string, and set it back in the drawer with the photo album on top and closed the drawer.

I sat the picture of Ben and his family on the stand where it had been and stood to leave. I turned as I reached the bedroom door to read what was etched in the wood of the rectangle frame. "Forever in my heart," it said. "It's perfect," I said and left the apartment.

Still wearing the sweatshirt, I pulled the hood up over my head and made a run for it down the stairs. The weather was much worse. The wind was blowing so hard the rain was coming down sideways and felt like pellets on my face that stung as I tried to shield myself by pulling the hood down over my face. "Oh my gosh!" I said as I closed the door behind me and threw back the hood. "Guess we are staying one more day … flights are cancelled," Aunt Abby said.

"Because of the weather?" I asked as I walked into the living room where Aunt Abby was sitting, still dripping from the soaking I had gotten on my way from the Carltons'.

"Yes, but there is something else going on," she said with a concern in her voice.

"What, Aunt Abby? What have you heard?" I asked her, wanting her to say something like "I've seen the lights too, it's not just you" or "I've talked to some of the neighbors and they have seen them glow in the water," but also fearing that she would say that. I had a feeling somewhere inside that was a sickening feeling, like being homesick and being far from home.

"I've been watching for a news report John says is on the Internet that there has been some sort of meteorite shower or something. NASA has reported some activity, pieces that have fallen into the Atlantic Ocean that may be the cause of the water heating up, killing all the fish and birds."

She was still talking, but I was not hearing anything else she was saying. My mind was trying to process what she was telling me. *Of course*, I thought to myself. *They would have had to have seen something.* They could not have just fallen out of the sky without something detecting it, but what if that was what it was, if it was pieces of rock? Wouldn't it burn up, like a falling star when it hit the ocean? What I had seen was still a burning light … lots of them under the water.

"They are going to have a news conference." I was jarred back to reality with a flash of lightning followed by a clap of thunder. "That is, if we don't lose power," Aunt Abby finished. I did not say a word as I ran up the stairs and into my room. I sat down at my desk and flipped open my laptop. As soon as my home page came up, the headlines read, "Solar Storm Causes Meteor Shower: Beaches Closed Up and Down the East Coast." "The Big One Yet to Come," read another piece. "Doomsday: Is This the End of the World?" another blogger had written.

I sat there as I read the words on the screen. It was like reading something out of a science book, talking about a star exploding and pieces falling through the earth's atmosphere. It was like falling stars that normally burn out before they hit the ground but like the one that had hit Earth in the past, causing the crater out west, but these had fallen into the water off the East Coast, the article explained. This possibly caused the rise in the water temperature, affecting the marine life and the weather. The article went on to say there was a possibility of a big chunk still out there. When and if it were to come into the Earth's atmosphere, it would be catastrophic. I shuddered as a chill ran down my back.

"This is it," I said out loud. "This is what Ben had meant when he said he had to tell them what's coming." My thoughts continued as I sat there at the desk, staring at the computer screen. The sun was destroying their planet, Ben had said. It was all starting to make sense. As crazy as it all seemed, it was making perfect sense to me. He had come here hoping to find a place they could survive. They had no other choice! They'd come here because their home was being destroyed. Whatever was in the water, it was not meteorites; it was … whatever Ben was.

I sat up and typed the website for NASA on my computer. I searched the second star from the moon. Proxima Centauri was its name. It was a vaporish, luminous star that had recently been discovered, recently being in the last one hundred years, it had gone on to read. Nothing unusual or out of the ordinary did I find about this star. Just a rock out there in space according to NASA, but I knew it was all connected in some way. As I scanned through the site reading all I could about this star that Ben had called home, I suddenly saw a posting from the night before.

"Proxima Centauri has disappeared from our constel-
lation. Gone," it boldly stated. Oh my God! I remembered
looking into the night sky, one minute seeing the light Ben
had pointed to, and then it was gone. Just like the article
had read. Gone, but it was not gone. Was it out there—or
at least a chunk of it? I closed my laptop and stood to go
downstairs.

"Ben, where are you?" I asked out loud as I walked out
of my bedroom door.

Aunt Abby was still glued to the TV as I sat down beside
her. She grabbed the throw from the back of the couch and
put it around me.

"You are still wet, Luvy," she said as she turned up the
volume on the remote. "This is it," she said as I looked at
the screen and saw the microphone set up and someone
had walked to the podium to speak.

I saw them. I could see their lips move, but it was like
I could not hear them. All I could think of was Ben. Where
was he? What was he doing? Had he gone to the authorities? What did they do? Did they believe him?

Aunt Abby put her hands to her mouth and then
touched my leg. "Oh no!" she said. I still could not focus. I
tried to read the ticker that was running across the bottom
of the screen. "Could hit the Earth's atmosphere as early
as two days from now ... missiles being readied ... where
could it hit? Not known yet ..." Just then, Aunt Abby's
phone rang.

"I'll get it," I said as I picked up her cell phone and
walked toward the kitchen so I could hear better. "It's

probably Mom anyway. Hey, this is Christi," I said as I answered her phone.

"Christi, honey, this is Nancy Carlton. Is Abby busy? I need to talk to her," she said with a desperate plea in her voice.

"She is watching the news, Mrs. Carlton. Can I give her a message? Is everything okay? Is Ben there?" I found myself asking her.

"He was, but … they've gone to the beach," she said.

"To the beach," I repeated. "Who? Ben?"

"Yes," she said. "Bob insisted he had to go in the water. I couldn't stop him, and neither could Ben, so he went after him. I don't know what he is doing. I don't know what to do." She was crying on the other end of the phone.

"Are they out front on the beach?" I asked her.

"No," she said. "He insisted they go toward the marsh. Should I call beach patrol? Ask Abby what I should do, Christi."

"You stay right there, Mrs. Carlton," I said to her. "We'll try to help Ben with Mr. Carlton, and we'll call patrol if we need to. That way, Mr. Carlton won't blame you. Don't worry. I'll call you back." I hung up the phone.

"It's Mrs. Carlton," I said as I laid her phone on the counter. "She needs my help with Mr. Carlton. I'll be back in a while. Don't worry. Call Mom and Dad for me. Tell them I love them. Love you, Aunt Abby."

I did not give her a chance to respond as I closed the door behind me. I ran down the steps and turned toward the marsh, the opposite direction from the Carltons'.

Forgive me! I thought as I had again lied to Aunt Abby, kind of. I was helping Mrs. Carlton with Mr. Carlton, after all. I pulled up the hood of the sweatshirt that I still had on and sprinted toward the marsh.

No one was out. Everyone was watching the news report, I thought. It was still midmorning, but the weather had made it as dark as evening would have been. Still an occasional flash of lightning, but the rain had subsided a bit. As I neared the marsh, I saw someone walking toward the beach. Not Ben or Mr. Carlton. This guy looked to be in a suit. *Out here in the rain in a suit?* I thought as I slowed up. I wasn't supposed to be out here either, so I did not want him to see me.

I looked ahead of him for any sight of Ben or Mr. Carlton. Just then, the guy started to run toward the beach. As I took off toward him, I could see two people in the distant haze. Ben and Mr. Carlton! I knew it had to be them. As I got to the edge of the dunes, I saw them.

"Hey!" the guy in the suit said. "You can't go in the water." He was speaking to Ben and Mr. Carlton, as they had turned to face him at the edge of the water. I crouched down in the tall sea grass as I watched Ben and Mr. Carlton turn back to the water without a word and start to walk into the waves.

"Stop!" the man said. "Stop now!" He took something out of his jacket.

Oh my God! I thought and gasped out loud as I saw it looked like a gun. I watched as Ben and Mr. Carlton walk out, and then … they were gone. I couldn't see them. I didn't see them dive under water. In the haze and drizzle, they were just gone!

The man in the suit ran to the water's edge. Looking out, up and down, he couldn't see them either. As he turned to go down the beach, not coming back toward the dunes, he hadn't seen the lights either. He looked back occasionally until I lost him in the haze. As soon as I was sure he wouldn't see me, I ran to the water's edge. *Tonight I will find out what and who you are,* I thought as I waded out into the waves and dove under the warm water and swam toward the lights.

Chapter Ten

The water felt so good. It was always the one place that I could get away from whatever was happening in my life and just be alone. I welcomed the quietness as I dove under the waves. I tried to put out of my mind thoughts of Aunt Abby and how disappointed she would be in me for lying to her and how she would freak out if she even thought I would go into the water, and it was still storming.

What are you thinking? I asked myself. *Are you crazy?* I surfaced the water, took a breath, wiped the salt water that was stinging my eyes, and looked around the surface of the water. Nothing. The haze of the storm had made the beach not visible from where I was. I couldn't tell how far out I had swum, and the swells were getting bigger as they pounded me.

"Now is my only chance! I have to know!" I said as I took a breath and dove under into the blackness of the water. I would surface only to take a quick breath and then under again as I tried to calculate in my mind the distance and the time it would take me to swim to where I had seen the lights. *This is it!* I thought. *I can't go out any further.*

I stopped and tried to get my bearings, but the swells were too big and the sky had become darker. As a flash of lightning lit up the sky, I could make out the outline of the pier and the faint lights at the end of it.

"Now!" I said as I sucked in a deep breath and slipped under the water. Down I swam, my eyes stinging from the salt water, looking for—? *I don't know*, I thought. I loved being alone in the water, but this time I felt I was not alone. I swam deeper and further out as I scanned for any sign of light. I could feel my lungs starting to burn, needing more air. *One more minute, just one more.* The same words I would tell myself when I trained. I stopped, looked again. It was more that I heard them before I saw them—muffled voices but definitely voices—and a haze of lights.

Christi, you need some air, I thought as I stared into the distance. I knew I needed air, but my mind was telling me this was my only chance to see what was going on. I swam closer to the voices coming from the glow.

"It's a choice we have to make." I froze in the water as I heard Ben's voice as clearly as if he was talking directly to me. *Is this possible?* I thought. *How can I be hearing this?* The impossible was again a reality, and I began to make out the individual light forms that made up the glow in the depths of the water.

"We can choose to stay here," another voice said.

117

"No! That is not an option!" It was definitely Ben.

"Wait," another voice said. "Let's listen to what Ion has to say."

Wait! Who? I thought.

"Thank you, Father," I heard Ben say. My mind was racing with so many questions as I heard him continue. "If we do nothing, they can't stop it. It's too big. Their weapons will only slow it down. Maybe destroy the whole continent. Maybe even worse."

"But we can survive in the water," came the objection from the voice I had heard before.

I was close enough that I could make out the forms of light. Some seemed to be balls of light, and others were humanlike, spiritlike, transparent light. *I need to get air,* my brain was telling me, but I couldn't move. My eyes were fixed on the light forms in the distance and the fact that somehow I was hearing their communication between each other.

"We know what our existence is doing to the ocean life. It could sustain us for a while, but it's affecting the weather on this planet also. So if what's left of our home doesn't destroy the whole planet, then changing the temperature of the ocean will. And we eventually may not survive anyway."

"We don't know that."

"Yes, I do know that!"

"Quiet!" I heard the voice of the one Ben had called Father say. "What would you have us do, my son?"

"That we use ourselves, our energy together, to deflect it. We came here hoping to find sustainable life, but at what cost, and for what? This planet will be destroyed too."

"How? How can we deflect it if their weapons can't?" came the defiant voice again.

"Silence!" the voice of authority said. "Continue," he said, much more calmly.

"We might not be able to, but if we combine our energy with that of their weapons, it might be enough. We have to try! Please, these people don't deserve this."

"May I speak?" someone asked.

Mr. Carlton? I thought as I recognized the voice of the man I had just seen go into the water with Ben.

"Yes, speak," came the answer.

"He is right—there is nothing to be gained here—and if we are successful, maybe the force will push our planet, what's left of it, away from the sun and on a track where we could possibly begin again. Isn't it possible?" There was a silence.

"Yes ... it is possible." The great voice answered.

"Don't listen to them. They are not thinking of us. They are thinking of those humans. They don't care that we may all be destroyed in this ... in this crazy mission. They are more concerned about the woman and the girl that Ion calls *princess*."

"Hey!" I yelled to myself at the defiant one's voice. Suddenly everything went completely silent. It was as if they had heard me. "Surface, Christi ... swim!" I cried to myself as I tried to make my ascent to the surface of the water. "Swim, damn it!" It was like I had lead tied around my ankles. "Go! Go! Go!" I swam, breaking the surface of the water as my lungs burst, gasping for air and spitting salt water.

Treading water, I looked around to get my bearings but found myself sinking under the water. "My legs!" I realized that I still had on the Michigan sweatshirt that I had taken from the apartment at the Carltons'. I struggled to get it up over my head and let it float away. *Don't fight it!* my mind was telling me. I broke the surface of the water again. "Ben!" I screamed, took a breath of air before I sank under the water, my legs unable to move and my arms not willing.

It's a dream, I thought. *Like all the others … he will save me.* As I sank into the depths of the water, I could see the lights coming closer. I could not move, half conscious, wanting to let the water in but somehow not able to.

"She's mine," I heard a female voice say.

"No!" the voice I knew was Ben's said, and then they were there, in front of me, encircling me. I could feel the heat that radiated from them, and the light lit up the darkness of the ocean floor. And from out of the midst of them came a form of shining light, more brilliant than the night he had unveiled himself to me. It was Ben. He seemed to float through the water and stopped in front of me. I could feel his energy all around me.

"I claimed her first," the female voice said. "She is part of me."

"You can't have her, Sariai," Ben said. "I won't let you."

It was as if I could feel his arm reach around behind him and pull me closer to him. Just then, a ball of light came out from the midst of them. A light so blinding I could not look at it.

Why am I not drowning? I thought as I closed my eyes.

"I will scan her."

"Father, please!" Ben pleaded.

I tried to open my eyes, but the light was so blinding I couldn't. I couldn't move. I felt Ben's arm move away from me. *Ben, what's happening?* I asked myself.

"Trust me," I heard him say as I felt his warmth fade, but it was soon replaced by an amazing sense of sunlight, a heat that warmed me to the core of my being.

A tingling ran through my body from my head to my toes. I tried to open my eyes slowly, squinting at first, but finding myself able to see. Looking around me, I saw that it was like I was in some kind of bubble ... a bubble of lights but a wonderful, beautiful, peaceful light. I felt no sense of fear, no sense of needing to get air into my lungs. "Let it in," I said to myself, like in my dreams. *I'm sorry, Aunt Abby*, I thought as I closed my eyes.

I felt the heat run through my veins like my blood was boiling. My lungs felt like they were going to burst, but somehow I was able to continue to hold my breath even though my mind was telling me, *It's okay. Let it in.* But then it was as if I had no control of my thoughts. My mind was racing, recounting events that I had not thought of for years—things that had happened when I was little, riding my bike, when I fell out of the tree in our backyard and broke my arm, my mom and dad, the divorce, coming here over the years with Aunt Abby, the events of this week. My whole life was flipping through my mind like a movie on some high-speed setting.

Stop it! I told myself, but images and events kept replaying in my mind, and then the warmth was gone, replaced with coldness of the ocean's depths. I opened my eyes to find the light that had surrounded me had moved away, but its brilliance was still there, far surpassing the many smaller lights that were there behind it. My body was suspended in the water somehow, like an anchor was weighing me down. I felt like I was losing consciousness but could still see and hear the thoughts of whatever was there with me in the water.

"She knows. How can we let her go?" I heard a voice say.

"She won't remember, Father. I can take it from her, but we have to let her go back. Please … do this for me." The words had come from Ben, who had again positioned himself in front of me. My mind was taking in what I was hearing, but I couldn't respond; it was numb. "Let me take her back. Then I will return," he continued.

"He won't come back," the defiant voice said.

"Father, I would not ask any of us to do something I am not committed to do myself. I will do as I say." There was a silence as I could do nothing but wait and listen.

"We knew when we left our home that all of us might not survive," the great voice said. "But we did, and maybe this is why. We have a purpose and a destiny. We always knew that, and now this is a chance to prove it. For all of our sakes, we will do this thing that you have asked of us. We will come together as one, and we will strike at the same instant as the missiles, and maybe we will salvage both of our worlds. Take her home and do what you must. We will gather and wait for you."

They were gone, just like that. The weight was gone from my ankles, and my lungs gave way. Water was coming in. I gulped in water as I swam toward the surface of the water. *Let it in*, I thought as once again my thoughts were my own. *It's okay*, I told myself. I was thrust through the water and broke the surface, spewing water, choking, fighting the waves. Ben was suddenly beside me, wrapping his arm around me. "Let me help you," he said as I put my arms around his neck and sleep came over me …

"But it's been a week," I heard Aunt Abby say. "The doctor says she is fine, just exhausted," she continued.

I opened my eyes and tried to focus on my surroundings. "Aunt Abby," I said as I squinted and tried to sit up.

"Luvy!" she said. "Oh, thank God!"

"Honey, how are you feeling?"

"Dad?" I asked as my eyes cleared and I could see my dad standing over me. "What are you doing here?" I asked him. "Aunt Abby? What's going on?" Again, I tried to sit up. I was woozy.

"Slowly," my dad said as he helped me sit up in my bed and propped a pillow behind my back.

"What happened?" I asked as I lay back against the pillow and closed my eyes to steady the dizziness.

"We will talk about that later," Aunt Abby said. "Right now, you just need to rest. I'll go get you some soup. You need to eat and get your strength back. I'll be right back." She leaned forward and kissed my forehead and got up and left the room.

"That's right, honey, you just need to rest," my dad said as he pulled the sheet up over my arms.

"Dad," I said. "I'm not a baby." And I pushed the sheet away from me. "Why are you even here?" I was irritated and not even sure why. Nothing was making sense.

"I came as soon as I could, honey," he said.

"Why? Did Aunt Abby call you?" My mind was racing, trying to remember what had happened before I woke up here in my bedroom.

"You almost drowned, honey. The boy staying at the Carltons' pulled you out of the water. He may have saved your life, and we are so grateful and thankful to him, but don't think about that now. You are going to be fine—that is all that matters now." He leaned and kissed my cheek. "I'll go get that soup and bring it to you. Love you, honey," he said as he stood and left the room.

I had heard what my dad had said, and I tried to focus my mind on what had happened. "Think!" I said to myself as I put my head in my hands. How could I have almost drowned? Why couldn't I remember? Mrs. Carlton. I raised my head; I was remembering. She had called … Mr. Carlton and Ben had gone to the marsh. She was worried. I was remembering the conversation I had had with her on the phone. I had left the house and followed them. There was someone else—a man—and then Ben and Mr. Carlton in the water. I had gone in after them.

What then? I asked myself. *Why can't you remember?* Frustrated, I threw back the sheet and stood to get out of the bed. Shakily, I steadied myself and walked to the window and pulled aside the curtain. The sun was beautiful. The water was a brilliant shade of blue, and there were people walking and playing and just lying on the sand. Gulls were swooping and scurrying along the sand, looking for crumbs left behind. Everything seemed so normal.

It was storming, I said to myself. *And the birds and the dead fish?* "It's been a week." I recalled what Aunt Abby had said. I let the curtain fall back into place. I went into the bathroom and ran hot water in the sink. I let the washcloth soak up the steamy water, wrung it out, and placed it on my face. It was so hot, and it felt so good. It felt familiar somehow, the warmth almost burning me. I hung the cloth on the rack and walked back into the bedroom.

"Ben?" I said as I saw him sitting in the chair beside my bed and blinked, only to find the chair empty as if I had imagined it. I looked around the room as if I might see him in the corner or sitting at the desk. My eyes stared at the desk where there was a piece of paper neatly folded lying on top of it, sitting against the mirror. Written on the front of it was the word *Princess.*

Chapter Eleven

"Here's your soup," I heard my dad say as he entered the room carrying a tray with a bowl of soup, a glass of water, what looked to be a cup of hot tea, and a vase with a flower in it. I opened the drawer of the desk and put the note inside and closed it. *I will read it later*, I told myself.

"Thanks, Dad," I said to him as he put the tray down on the desk. "Your mom will be here soon—with the travel restrictions and all, she's just leaving the airport."

"Dad ..." I whined. "What is all the fuss? I'm fine!"

"You are fine. She just needs to see you. I understand that. We both just needed to see for ourselves that you are okay," he said as he put his arms around me and hugged me tightly to him.

Travel restrictions? I thought as I remembered that Aunt Abby had had trouble booking a flight. "The star?"

I said as I was starting to recall the news from—I guess it would have been over a week ago. "What?" I was starting to panic.

"It's okay, honey," my dad said. "Everything is fine. It was deflected. Everything is back to normal. Just flights cancelled for a couple of days, and then delays caused by the huge backup. Your mom will be so excited to see you. That's enough talk! You need to eat and then rest. She'll be up as soon as she gets here. Now eat!" He hugged me tightly again and walked out of the room, closing the door behind him.

I took the note out of the desk drawer and walked over to the window, where the sunlight shining through felt good on my face. I closed my eyes for a moment and let the warmth flood over me. Suddenly everything was dark, so dark I couldn't see. I couldn't focus my eyes. I blinked to clear the salt water that was stinging my eyes. A blinding light replaced darkness with an intense heat, burning almost. *Christi*, I said to myself, and my eyes opened to find myself standing at my window. "What just happened?" I said out loud as I walked around the edge of the bed and sat down on the end of it. *Was I about to black out?* I thought to myself, remembering I had felt hot and everything had gone black when I passed out after falling and breaking my arm when I was ten. I reached for the glass of water on the tray and took a drink of it. I set it back on the tray and unfolded the piece of paper, and I smiled as I read the words that were written inside:

I know how much you hate it when I call you that. Do you believe in fate? I do. That we all have a destiny, and no matter how hard we may try to change it, some things are just how they are meant to be. Even though we may not be able to stop things from happening, we can affect the results. And that's why we are all here … to see what we do with what's given to us. I am better for having met you. Don't forget me. I hope you find your Prince Charming … isn't that the destiny of a princess?

"He sat with you for hours at the hospital, you know," I heard Aunt Abby say as I looked up and saw her standing in the doorway. I folded the note and placed it on the desk beside the tray of food and walked over to her and put my arms around her. "We were all scared for a while, Luvy. Here, why don't you lie back down?" she said as we walked back to the bed. She threw back the sheet and fluffed my pillow. As I lay back on the bed, she covered me up with the sheet.

"I can't remember, Aunt Abby. Tell me what happened. I need to know." I was pleading with her.

"Ben came carrying you into the house saying, 'Call 911!' You were breathing but unconscious. He said you had come into the water trying to help him with Mr. Carlton. I didn't know until later that when Nancy called earlier that evening, you had gone to the marsh after them. Luvy, you know you should never have gone out!"

"I know I should not have gone. I'm sorry," I said to her.

"You're okay now, that's all that matters," she said and patted my hand.

"I remember all that. What happened in the water? I'm a good swimmer. I don't know what happened." I was trying to recall the events after having seen Ben and Mr. Carlton vanish into the water. *Wait*, I thought. *They disappeared.*

"I guess Bob was determined he was going into the water—no stopping him," she continued. "Even though Ben tried, they struggled in the water. Ben says you must have seen them struggling and came to help, but the storm was bad and the waves were so strong. Bob was so determined to go … that Ben had to make a choice. He let go of Bob, and somehow, thank God, he made it back to shore with you. He stayed right beside you, never left your side until the doctor at the hospital said you would be okay."

"How long was I in the hospital?" I asked her as my mind was trying to place all the events she had just recounted for me.

"Four days. You would wake—only to go back to sleep again. All tests were fine. They said you just needed rest, so we brought you home."

"How long was Ben there?"

"Until the tests came back, all that night. He was very concerned, Luvy. Very nice young man—we owe him a lot," she said.

"Where is he? Is he still at the Carltons'?"

"I haven't seen him since that night at the hospital. I did ask Nancy, and she has not seen him. His things are still in the apartment. Nancy's worried about him with what happened to his family and now what's happened to Bob."

"What about Mr. Carlton?" I asked. "Is he okay?" I looked at Aunt Abby as her expression changed to one of sadness.

"He didn't make it out of the water, Luvy. They found his sweatshirt, but that was all. He is still missing."

His sweatshirt? I thought to myself as I remembered having grabbed Mr. Carlton's sweatshirt from the garage apartment that day. I remembered taking it off ... when I was in the water. I had felt myself sinking. *Let it in*, I remembered telling myself, and then there was Ben pulling me up and out of the water.

"Yes!" I said out loud. "Ben did save my life." I glanced at the note I had left on my desk.

"Enough for now," Aunt Abby said. "Your mom called, and she is almost here. Do you feel like coming down?"

"I think I want to shower first ... or maybe I'll soak for a while, then I'll be down."

"Okay," she said as she stood to leave. "Eat your soup." She smiled as she closed the bedroom door.

I got up out of the bed and walked over to the desk, sat down, and took a bite of the chicken noodle soup. What Aunt Abby had said had made sense. I had followed Ben and Mr. Carlton into the water. I did remember sinking under the waves and my lungs filling with water, feeling like they would burst, that burning feeling. I did remember surfacing and calling out to Ben, only to sink under the water again.

I thought of Mr. Carlton. I felt sad for Mrs. Carlton. Maybe I should have called 911 before I went out that day. Maybe it would have turned out differently. No, it would not have made a difference, I told myself as I walked into the bathroom and closed the door behind me. I felt sorry for Mrs. Carlton, but somehow I knew that Mr. Carlton had done just exactly what he had set out to do; nothing or no one would have prevented it. I was sure of it. *Fate*, I thought as I recalled the words Ben had written on the note he had left for me. I turned the water on and started to undress as the water began to fill the tub.

It's been a week since I've had a shower! Ugh! I thought as I stood naked and looked into the full-length mirror that hung on the bathroom door. I had been out of the water too long. It would feel good.

The water felt cool as I stepped into the tub. I adjusted the dial to Hot as I eased myself into the chilly water that had filled the tub a few inches. I leaned my head back against the back of the tub and stared at the ceiling. *I don't believe in fate*, I said to myself. It wasn't fate that my parents had gotten divorced. It wasn't fate that my mom had moved across the country, and how could it be fate that I had just lost a week of my life? "And where are you?" I said out loud to the ceiling. "How could you just leave? Moron," I said as I turned off the water and slid underneath. The water was hot, and it was soothing to my skin as I relaxed and began to count ... *One thousand one, one thousand two, one thousand three ...*

"We have a purpose and a destiny," I heard a voice in my head say. "Let me take her home." It was Ben's voice. "I will return, Father."

I burst out of the water. "I remember!" I said as I replayed in my mind the events of the week. I remembered Ben pointing to the star, the star that had broken apart, the star that had been his home. I remembered the lights in the water. I remembered following Ben and Mr. Carlton into the water, seeing them, hearing them. I remembered it all!

I sat there knowing it had happened just as I heard them say it. Had they been a part of deflecting the portion of the star that threatened this planet? "I have to know!" I said as I jumped out of the water, grabbed a towel, wrapped it around me, and ran into the bedroom. I grabbed my computer from the desk, sat down on the bed, and logged on.

"In Case You Missed It ... See the Lights" was the headline that popped up on the news screen. I clicked on the video and watched as what appeared to be a missile light up the sky with a flame surrounding it and then a second trailing behind it; it was like seeing a comet. These clusters of light were going upward, coming together in a magnificent ball of glowing light. As the distance of the two became greater, they became smaller on the video, but the camera was still able to track them, and then there was an explosion of light. The screen captured the night sky, and then it was gone. The video was over as I sat there in silence, knowing what I had just watched was much more than missiles launched at a meteor. "NASA Denies Launch of Two Missiles," another headline read. "Optical Illusion?" another wrote. "What Is NASA Not Telling Us?" another article read.

"We could begin again," I remembered Mr. Carlton saying. He had chosen his destiny, and so had Ben, I thought, as a wave of sadness came over me. I closed my computer and lay back on my bed. "I can make her forget." His words echoed in my mind. I sat up and reached for the note, opened it, and scanned the words he had written: "Don't forget me …"

"You wanted me to remember," I said out loud.

"Christi?" I heard my mom's voice as she knocked on my bedroom door. "Honey?" She said as she walked over to me. "Are you okay?" she asked as she put her arms around me and hugged me tightly.

"I'm fine, Mom," I said. "You didn't need to come all the way here. I'm fine." I walked over to the dresser drawer and took out my underclothes and a pair of shorts and a top.

"Yes, I did need to be here. I'm just sorry I couldn't get here sooner," she said as I pulled on a pair of shorts I had taken from the drawer. "It was terrible not being able to get to you with everything that was happening and not knowing. Oh my goodness, Christi! What is that?"

I had dropped my towel as I fastened my bra and reached for my shirt. "What?" I turned to see what she was asking about.

"Your skin, honey. Are you sunburned?"

I looked down and saw that my arms, my legs, and my stomach were bright red. "Oh, I guess the water was a little hot in my bath. It's okay, see," I said as I patted my arms and tummy. "I'm fine."

"A little hot, honey? That's a severe burn."

"Mom!" I yelled at her. "Stop hovering! I'm fine!" I snapped.

"I'm sorry," she said. "I'm just worried about you."

"No, I'm sorry," I said and hugged her. "But don't worry. I'm fine. I promise." I finished getting dressed. "How's Poppy?" I asked her as I buttoned my shirt, picked up the towel I had dropped on the floor, and walked into the bathroom to hang it on the rack. I pulled a brush out of the drawer and started to brush my hair.

"He's doing okay. He's just not going to get much better, but he has some good days. We are getting settled in— you will love it there."

"Mom …" I said as I looked into the mirror. I had had a lot of sunburns from my days at the beach, but this was bad. My face was blood red.

"Okay, we won't bring it up again," I heard her say as I put my index finger on my forehead and saw my skin peel back under the pressure of it. I didn't feel it, but the sight of it made me nauseous. I steadied myself and then carefully moved the skin back into place and brushed my bangs over to the side to cover it.

"Mom," I said as I walked back into the bedroom and sat down on the bed. "Do you believe in fate? That everything happens for a reason?"

"Honey, if you are talking about Mr. Carlton, there was nothing more that you could have done. Everyone, including Mrs. Carlton, knows that," she said as she sat down on the bed beside me. "Are you sure you're okay?"

"Christi," my dad said as he opened the door and peeked his head in. "There is someone here to see you if you are up to it."

"Ben?" I asked as I jumped to my feet and ran past him into the hallway.

"No," he answered. "A detective. He wants to ask you a few questions, but only if you feel up to it." My heart sank as I turned to him.

"Will I have to talk to him eventually anyway?"

"It doesn't have to be now," he said. "I can ask him to come back."

"No, let's get it over with," I said as I turned to go down the hall to the stairway with my dad and mom following behind me. "Am I in trouble?" I asked as I entered the living room from the stairs.

"No," my dad and Aunt Abby said at the same time.

"No one is in trouble," the detective said as he stood and turned to face me. "I'm Detective Baker." He walked over to me and put out his hand. I shook his hand and walked past him to sit on the couch. "Do you feel like answering a few questions, Miss Randolph?" he asked.

"I don't remember anything, but you can ask," I lied. I lied because I remembered everything. He was the guy I had seen at the marsh that day in the same suit he had on now. He had warned Ben and Mr. Carlton not to go into the water. I had watched him walk away.

"I first want to say how thankful we are that you are going to be fine. Can I ask why you went into the water? You did know there were warnings and postings not to go into the water? Didn't you?" he asked.

I thought for a moment and then answered him. "I knew it was posted not to go in the water, but I don't remember what caused me to go in."

"Can you think back? Did you see a struggle? Did you see Ben and Mr. Carlton go into the water? Any sign of them struggling? Is that why you went in? Did you see them struggling in the water?" He was bombarding me with questions.

"Ben saved my life. Are you accusing him of something else?" I asked him in a defiant tone.

"Any kind of struggle could mean Ben was trying to save Mr. Carlton, not anything more than that," he said, looking at me for a response.

"I don't remember anything," I said to him and looked out the front window.

"I think that's all," my dad said.

"Okay," the detective said as he turned to leave. "If you remember anything at all, let us know."

"Why were you there?" I asked him as he got to the door.

"Mrs. Carlton called, saying her husband was determined he was going into the water and had gone out. She wanted us to check the beach. Funny, though—I didn't mention that I was the one who responded," he said as he stood in the open door, looking at me. "Thanks for your time. Be sure to put something on that burn."

I turned away as my dad closed the door behind him.

Chapter Twelve

I sat there on the couch and drew my legs up to my chest and put my arms around them and laid my head on my knees.

"She had the same rash when Ben brought her in that night," Aunt Abby said.

"She said the water was a little too hot in her bath. I think she scalded her skin a little. We should put some aloe or something on it." My mom was opening the cabinets in the kitchen, looking for something that suited her. I could hear the rustling of things being moved.

"I don't understand why they were here questioning her. She almost drowned." It was my dad's turn now. "Shouldn't they be questioning this Ben guy? He's the only one who really knows what happened."

"They questioned him that night at the hospital," Aunt Abby told my dad. "They are trying to figure out why she went into the water to begin with, I guess. She had to be trying to help. That's what Ben said. She wouldn't have gone in for any other reason. It was storming, and … she just would have listened to the warnings if she had not had a very good reason for going in."

"I'd like to talk to this guy myself," my dad said. "See what he says."

"Would you guys stop it!" I blurted out. "You are talking like I'm not even in the room. Does it matter why I went into the water? Shouldn't it only matter that Ben saved my life? He is not the villain here, and besides, Mr. Carlton knew exactly what he was doing." There was a momentary silence as I stood, and all three were looking at me.

"Luvy, are you remembering something?" Aunt Abby said and walked toward me.

I walked past her and out of the living room, ran up the stairs, and into my room. I leaned against the door. *Where are you?* I asked myself, knowing but not willing to accept the answer.

"Don't worry … trust me." They were words I had heard Ben say before, but the words in my mind seemed so real.

"Ben?" I looked around the room, expecting to see him. I raised my wrist and traced the letters on the bracelet that my mom had given me. I smiled as I remembered the events of the morning Aunt Abby and I had left for our trip.

"Luvy?" I heard Aunt Abby's voice as she knocked softly on my door. "Can I come in?" I turned and turned the doorknob to open the door. She walked past me, and I closed the door behind her. "We didn't mean to upset you, Luvy ... we're sorry for being insensitive."

I walked over to her and laid my head on her chest and put my arms around her. "I love you so much," I said to her.

"To the moon and back," she said as she hugged me to her. "Oh, Luvy ..." she sighed. "These two weeks were sure not what we expected. I'm so thankful that you are okay." She kissed the top of my head. "It will be good to get home and back to normal." She loosened her hug, and I stepped back and sat down on the side of the bed. She sat down beside me and tucked my hair behind my ear. "We are leaving in the morning. Your mom and dad want Dr. Lee to examine you ... just to be sure everything is okay."

"I'm fine," I said as I got up and walked over to the window, pulling the curtain back.

"I know you are, Luvy. They are just being cautious." I stood there, looking out at the beautiful blue water.

"Did Ben say anything before he left the hospital? Did he say he was leaving?" I asked her, still looking out the window.

"He apologized for not seeing you before you got into the water. Maybe he could have prevented what happened to you. He gave me the note. He kissed you."

I turned from the window. "What?" I asked her.

She smiled as she said, "I smiled when I saw that he had written *Princess* on the front of the note. I told him that Prince Charming, after he rescues the princess, kisses her and she would awaken ... and he did, but you did not wake up. He left after that."

I raised my fingers to my lips. I remembered the feeling I had when he kissed me that night on the dunes. I tingled inside.

"It was worth a try." She smiled. "He seemed to care more than a lifeguard you had just met, Luvy." She seemed to be asking a question more than making a statement.

"Remember when I dropped my tray at the airport and lost my bracelet?" I asked her and rubbed the many bracelets on my wrist.

"Of course," she said.

"He is the one who bumped into me—Ben—he caused me to drop my tray, and he had my bracelet when I went back to look. Isn't that weird?"

She just sat there and looked at me.

"Don't you remember him now? He was right there beside you when he knocked into me." I waited for her to recall what had happened in the security line at the airport. "Surely you remember him?"

"Luvy, I remember you tripping, but I didn't see anyone bump into you," she said.

"He was trying to help us pick them up—the bracelets. I yelled at him ... Aunt Abby?"

"I'm sorry, Luvy. Maybe things are running together for you." She stood and reached out to touch my arm.

141

"Why don't you rest a while? We'll check on you in a little while." She kissed my cheek and left the room, closing the door behind her.

I laid down on the bed, turned over on my side, and curled my legs up. My mind was racing. I couldn't separate what was real in my mind. *It happened*, I thought, I was sure of it, but why did Aunt Abby not see him? She had to have. But she hadn't seen the lights either. "Maybe I am crazy," I said out loud and closed my eyes.

It was evening when I woke. I had slept without any dreams. I walked into the bathroom and ran cold water in the sink. I splashed it on my face and reached for the towel that hung on the wall. As I patted my face dry, I looked in the mirror. The burn had faded. I looked at my hands and legs that just a few hours ago were beet red—now they were normal. I leaned forward and looked at the spot where my skin had peeled back on my forehead. It was gone. "Hmmm," I said and laid the towel on the sink.

I stood there and looked at myself in the mirror. I seemed different somehow. I again leaned in toward the mirror and examined my face. I stepped back and held my hands out and looked at them. They looked almost translucent. I glanced back into the mirror and then back at my hands. Suddenly, everything began to blur. I steadied myself and looked again at my hands, finding them normal. "Maybe I do need to eat something," I said as I walked out of the bathroom and left the bedroom to go downstairs.

"Hey, honey," my dad said as I walked down the stairs into the kitchen.

"Hey," I said as I grabbed a banana from the counter and started to peel it. He was watching *Sports Center.* "Where are Mom and Aunt Abby?" I asked as I walked into the living room.

"Your mom laid down for a nap a few hours ago, and Abby's upstairs—packing I think," he said, still watching whatever sports news that was on. I walked past him and out the door to the porch and sat down on the swing. I saw my dad stand and look out long enough to see I had not gone far and then go back to his TV program.

The sound of the waves was relaxing as I started the swing in motion. I looked out over the water as night was starting to fall. I looked out at the sky beyond the waves. The moon was visible but not yet dark enough to see the stars. "How will I ever know?" I said out loud as the screen door opened. "Mrs. Carlton!" I was surprised to see her standing there.

"Can I sit with you?" she asked as she sat down a bag she was carrying.

"Sure," I said as I scooted to one side of the swing.

"I'm leaving early in the morning, and I wanted to see you before I left. I wanted to make sure you are okay," she said as she patted my leg and looked at me.

"Oh, Mrs. Carlton. I'm fine. How are you doing though?" I asked her and put my hand on hers.

"I will be," she said as her tone and face saddened. "I lost him several months back, but being here … gave me hope that he was coming back to me. I think he was afraid he would slip back into a place he didn't want to be again. I think he made a choice that day, in a place that he loved, doing what he wanted to do—his way." Tears ran down her cheek as she wiped them away.

"I think you are right. He did make a choice, and he must have thought he was doing the right thing—for you and him. I know it." She managed a half smile and stood.

"Ben left something for you," she said as she picked up the bag. "I hoped I could get it to you before I had to leave."

"When did you see him? Was he here?" I asked.

"He left the day after the accident. Didn't take any of his stuff, but he asked me to give you this." She handed the bag to me. "I don't know what I would have done without Ben. We wouldn't have made this trip without him. I wouldn't have been able to do it myself. Maybe we should have stayed home, but Bob loved it here, so I can't think about the what-ifs. I'm so glad you are okay. It would have been unbearable if something had happened to you too," she said as she turned to leave.

"I know it may sound strange, Mrs. Carlton, but you should be proud of your husband. Don't ever think anything less than that." She smiled as she opened the screen door. "Oh, Mrs. Carlton, did the three of you fly down together?"

"Fly? No, we drove down. Wish we had now—I really dread the drive back."

"All three of you? Ben drove down with you? He didn't fly down and meet you here?"

"He came with us. We couldn't have managed without him. I hope he is okay. This was very hard on him. His family drowned here too, you know. Wherever he is, I pray he is okay." She walked into the house where Aunt Abby had joined my dad in the living room, and they sat down with Mrs. Carlton and began to talk with her.

That's impossible, I thought to myself. *He was there in the airport. I know it. How can that be?* I sat there on the swing, trying to sort out in my mind an explanation, but there was none. I sat the bag on the swing beside me and reached inside. I pulled out a box, the same box I had seen in the nightstand in Ben's apartment.

I slowly opened the lid. In it were the contents I had seen before. Letters, pictures, things from his past. On top was the picture frame I had left there, with the picture of his family in it. There was a note stuck to it that read "I'm counting on you to bury the past for me, but it will remain forever in our hearts." I put the box back into the bag and walked into the house.

"What time are we leaving in the morning?" I asked.

"By ten," Aunt Abby said.

"Good. I want to run before we leave."

"I don't think you should, honey," my dad said.

"Dad, it's the last morning here …"

"Let her run. She'll be fine," Aunt Abby said to my dad.

"I'm going out early," I said as I started up the stairs.

"See you this summer, Mrs. Carlton."

"Christi," she said as I looked back at her. "Thank you."

I smiled as and went up the stairs to my room. The night would not be over soon enough. At first light, I would go to the marsh. I knew what he wanted me to do. I pulled back the curtains and looked at the black water. No lights, not even a boat in the distance. I stared at the waves, expecting to see something, anything, but there was nothing, just white foam from the waves. Funny how normal now, somehow, seemed not normal. Even though Ben was not here, he was still finding a way to communicate with me. I would do this for him, and I knew he would know somehow that I had done what he asked. I couldn't chance going out tonight with my mom and dad both here; it would have to wait until morning. "After all, he's gone," I said. I took one last look at the star-filled night sky and let the curtain fall back into place.

Between searching the Internet for information on the events of the last week and my mom and dad and Aunt Abby coming in every hour to check on me, sleep was not an option for me. Even though I would not have slept anyway, the morning was almost here. I closed my computer and looked at the clock on my nightstand. It read 4:30 a.m. I hoped staring at it would will it to move faster. It would not be light until 6:00 a.m. *Ugh, I can't wait any longer*, I thought as I threw back the covers and grabbed my shoes and somehow managed to get them tied, pulled my sweatshirt over my head, and picked up the tote that I had put the box in.

I had emptied the collection of scarves and ribbons from a plastic container and placed the box containing the memories of Ben's childhood, of his parents, and his sister inside it. I had fought the urge to go to the dunes all night. It was not just that I wanted to do what Ben had asked me to for him; it was more that I felt like I had to go. It was a longing almost.

I opened my door; everyone was still sleeping. The light was on in the kitchen, so it was casting enough light up the stairs that I could see as I half ran down the stairs and slipped out the front door. I hope Mrs. Carlton had not locked the storage room under the garage. I would again use their shovel. "Thank you," I said as I found it unlocked and the shovel where I had seen it before. I picked it up, shut the door, and turned up the driveway to the road to the marsh.

I walked and half ran down the paved road, holding the container close to my chest and the shovel in the other hand. It was dark at the end of the road that ran in front of the beachfront houses all the way to the entrance of the dunes. I leaned the shovel against me and took my cell phone out of my back pocket. I hit the flashlight app and put the handle of the shovel under my arm as I began to make my way across the dunes. I knew where I needed to go. I hoped I could find the spot in the darkness. The sound of the waves grew louder as I came closer to the edge of the dunes.

I could see the whitecaps against the darkness of the water. I stood on one of the dunes and looked out at the vastness of the ocean. The sun would be coming up soon. I turned and directed the light along the sand until I found the spot I was looking for. I would bury the box of memories alongside the spot that we had buried Sam and the pelican. This spot made everything that happened real to me.

The bad and the good, I thought as I remembered not too far from this spot was where I had discovered who Ben was, and as we lived through the events of that week, I found out who he was inside. I smiled as I thought of the times I had called him a moron—I wished I could take it back. I sat down the bag and began to dig deep enough. I took the box out of the container and kneeled down and opened the box. I looked through the pictures, letters, pieces of lives cut too short.

Why? I thought. *Fate? Destiny?* Tears welled up in my eyes and spilled over as I looked at the frame I had placed his family's picture in. I ran my fingers over the words that were carved in the frame—*Forever in My Heart.* I put the lid on the container and leaned down to put it in the hole I had dug. I stood and picked up the shovel and began to scrape the sand back into the hole.

This place had to have had a special meaning to him, I thought as I packed the sand down with the shovel. *He's leaving everything that meant anything to him ... here.* I looked out over the marsh and turned to look out over the water. Tears ran down my cheeks. "I won't forget," I said out loud as I picked up the bag along with the shovel and stepped down from the dunes onto the beach.

I would walk back along the beach. The sun was breaking over the water. It was beautiful. I wiped away the tears and ran down the beach to Mrs. Carlton's. People were beginning to make their way out to the beach to collect shells and to watch the sun rise. I walked up the steps to the walkway of the Carltons'. I went down the side steps to the storage room. I set the shovel inside and closed the door.

"One last run," I said as I headed back to the beach. I threw the bag in the trash can at the edge of the dunes. I ran along the water's edge toward the pier. The sound of the gulls filled the morning air. Sandpipers scurried on the sand to find their first meal of the day. I looked out over the water as I ran, hoping to see a dolphin fin.

Nothing yet, but I knew they were there. Fishermen were setting their lines on the pier. The birds were already beginning to congregate and hover over the whole area, waiting for an opportunity for a fish or a worm. I stopped at the base of the pier and let the sun flood over my face. For a moment, I let my mind drift.

What if things had gone differently? I thought. *What if the wrong choice had been made? What if . . .*

"Christi." I heard a familiar voice.

I opened my eyes and saw Mrs. Jackson coming toward me. Not just Mrs. Jackson—she had a puppy that was running in and out of the waves. It was stopping to chomp at the foam and then running the length that the leash would allow. I ran to meet them, knelt down, and was welcomed with wet paws and licks as the pup jumped all around and on me.

"Hey, you!" I said to the pup, and I ruffed up its fur. I smiled up at Mrs. Jackson.

"Her name is Sami, short for Samantha," she said.

"Oh! I'm so glad you decided to get another dog! She is great!" I said as I stood and Sami chased the foam on the waves.

"Well, I really didn't decide. Ben did for me," she said. "He just brought me the pup. Said she needed a home. He has a way ... how could I say no?" She leaned down and scooped up the pup, who rewarded her with wet kisses all over her face.

"She's beautiful. She will be a great friend. How long have you had her?" I asked.

"He brought her by before he left ... a week ago, I guess. I'm so glad the both of you are okay, and I'm glad I got to see you—didn't think I would."

"I know. We are leaving today." I hugged her before starting on down the beach. "I'll look forward to seeing you and Sami this summer. Love your hat!" I waved as I regained my stride. I was always sad when we left the beach, but this time was different. It felt like I was leaving a part of me here. This place would never be the same because of what happened here, because of what I knew.

I looked out over the water. "There!" I said out loud. I stopped to watch the dolphin ease in and out of the water. *It didn't take long for nature or the tourists to get back to normal,* I thought as I stood there watching the gracefulness of this beautiful creature and hearing the laughter and loud voices of people as they began to spill onto the beach with their chairs, umbrellas, coolers, and kids in tow.

I walked along the edge of the water, letting the waves splash against my calves. I was in no hurry to get back. I was in no hurry to leave this place. I walked past a couple whose kids were building a sand castle, already enjoying their time here. I instinctively felt for my bracelet; I rubbed my hand on the mass that covered my wrist. I looked down when I did not feel the familiar metal of the bracelet my mom had given me.

"Oh no!" I said out loud as I began to run down the beach toward the dunes. It had to have come off when I was there digging in the sand. "Please let it be there!" I ran past the beach house. Aunt Abby was on the porch drinking coffee. I waved as I ran by. "I'll be right there!" I yelled as I kept running. I ran onto the marsh to the spot where I had dug just a couple of hours earlier. I fell down on the sand and frantically began to feel around, digging with my hands through the sand.

"I have it." I froze as I heard the words. I stood but couldn't bring myself to turn toward the direction of Ben's voice. "I knew you would come back for it." It was the same words he had spoken to me that morning at the airport. I turned slowly toward his voice, expecting that it was all in my mind. I saw him standing there with my bracelet dangling from his fingers, holding the box I had buried. I blinked, fearing that when I opened my eyes he would be gone, but he was there.

"I don't know if you are real or not. Are you just in my mind?" I asked him, as I stood there staring at him. "I've seen you when you're not there. I hear your voice inside my head." He walked over to me, took my wrist, and gently latched the bracelet, and without letting go of my hand, he placed it on his heart. With his other hand, he traced the line of my chin and tipped my face toward his as he leaned forward and kissed me. I felt weak in the knees as I put my arms around him and returned his kiss.

"I didn't think I would ever see you again," I said as tears streamed down my cheeks.

"I couldn't leave," he said as he wiped my tears. "And I didn't want to." He ran his hand down the side of my face.

"But I thought—?" I said.

"Shhh …" he said and kissed my cheek.

"I remember it all, Ben." He looked at me.

"I was counting on it," he said.

"I'm not the same. I won't ever be the same."

"Me either," he said as he pulled me to him.

"What now?" I asked him as I stepped back and looked at him.

"It is unfinished here," he said. "I'm not the only one who stayed behind. But you have to go now. Keep this for me." He handed me the box.

"But what about you?" I asked him.

"I'll find you," he said and kissed me lightly. "Trust me."

I turned to walk away. "Why me?" I asked him.

He paused for a moment then said, "Why not you?"

"Ben?" I said as I turned back to where he stood. He was gone. I looked at the bracelet on my wrist. I turned to walk back down the beach. I didn't know what life held in my future, but one thing was for sure—it would never be the same.

I looked out over the water; dolphins were playing. I felt a burning inside my body and a desire to be in the water; at least some things would never change. "I love the water," I said to myself. I had more questions than answers, but Aunt Abby was waiting on me; we were going home. I turned and looked once more at the dunes where Ben had stood.

"Trust me," he had said. "I will find you."

I smiled as I ran down the beach toward the house.

About the Author

Married for thirty-eight years to her soul mate, Gail has two fur babies (Simba and Nala) and a family she adores. She's a lover of sci-fi and fantasy novels, enjoys spending time at the beach, and loves big, floppy hats; long, flowy skirts; and Reese's Peanut Butter Cups. When she was a young girl, she loved to look at the stars and imagine she could do anything and become whatever she wanted to be; she just needed to believe in herself and keep on dreaming.

CPSIA information can be obtained at www.ICGtesting.com
Printed in the USA
LVOW11s1044061016

507566LV00002B/3/P